Arrangements
by Arial

Gregory Speers

Copyright © 2024 Gregory Speers
All rights reserved
First Edition

PAGE PUBLISHING
Conneaut Lake, PA

First originally published by Page Publishing 2024

ISBN 979-8-89157-779-4 (pbk)
ISBN 979-8-89157-797-8 (digital)

Printed in the United States of America

— *Note from the Author* —

WRITING IS MY THERAPY. When I wrote this book, the night was truly dark, and I am happy to report that the dawn has come. This book was an absolute Baja Blast to write, and I hope reading it makes you feel fly like a G6. If it doesn't, please feel free to reach out and yell obscenities at me. This book is dedicated to the thousands working in the shadows of night to ensure the world remains intact in the morning. We stand alone together.

Nihil vivit aut frustra moritur.

— *Chapter 1* —

Another Day in Paradise, and Other Canned Phrases

"Wʜᴀᴛ?" I ʏᴇʟʟᴇᴅ.

The twenty-two-year-old blond looked like she had just got done raiding her grandmother's closet, with her baggy pants and large brimmed hat. But in 2023 that was the essence of high fashion.

She pushed her fingers out into a number two, and I saw her mouth.

"Two more."

The music's bass line thudded against my eardrums, threatening to take the last of my hearing. The Sarajevo Night Club was packed for a Saturday night, and nothing about the evening's progression would indicate that the gaggle fuck of patrons would be thinning out anytime soon.

I knew what drink she wanted. I was disinclined to provide her with fast, expert service because of how she treated my coworker, B-Don, moments earlier. Expert service. What a joke. I had only been a bartender for the last three months. How fucking expert could it be?

I reached into the cooler and handed the nice, older gentleman to her right the same beer he had been drinking for the last two hours. I rang it into the point-of-sale system while the entitled harpy to his right attempted to yell over the din.

I ignored her and grabbed my tin shaker. I began loading it with the sugary ingredients for two lemon drops. I shook the drinks while she tried to make small talk with me over the bar. I nodded my head and smiled. She laughed. I laughed. She thought I found her funny. I had no idea what she said. Thus, the game was played.

I strained the drink into the two glasses on the bar.

She leaned in close and screamed, "Actually, can you make one more?"

I bit back a frustrated response. I poured another shot in the shaker and made a third lemon drop. She took them and handed them one by one to the other twenty-somethings next to her. They started recording themselves taking the shots for their social-media posts. I moved on to the next customer.

The night turned into a blur of motion, light, and noise. I found my rhythm and stayed on beat. I sat down three glasses to make Long Islands. I finished the drinks. A girl caught my eye at the end of the bar. My fingers found nothing but condensation as I grabbed the drinks, and they crashed violently to the floor. Broken glass and liquor decorated my boots. All eyes in front of the bar and behind it shifted to me. I turned a shade of red I didn't know existed.

The other bartenders looked at me and started slow clapping. I took a bow and tried to play it off. Then the intrusive thoughts came.

You can't do anything right, you piece of shit. Two or three more of those and you're back on the street where you belong.

I tried to shake off my inner monologue, but it decided it wasn't done yet.

You couldn't make the grade in high school. You couldn't make it in college. Why should you start making it now?

I grabbed three more glasses and remade the drinks.

Come on, you dumpster fire, you can't even make a Long Island. Give up and go back to the homeless village.

Stuffing my deeply flawed self-talk down where the cancer grows, I got a clearer look at the girl at the end of the bar. She was younger than me, probably twenty-six or twenty-seven, a suit of gray wool, and a quaint silver necklace with a small decorative dagger pendant adorned her neck. Her angular face was framed by jet-black hair, and infernal green eyes sliced into me. Something about her said upper-middle class, probably in charge of something.

I went to hand off the Long Islands to the large Hawaiian-shirt-clad man, who by now had become impatient for his order.

I handed him the drinks. "Thirty-six dollars, please."

He threw his hands around like he was an extra on the sopranos. "Fuck you. I'm not paying for these. You made me wait like ten fucking minutes."

I gently placed my hand on his and seductively leaned as far over the bar as my stature would allow.

I got close to his ear and said, "Sir, do you see that man over there?"

I pointed at a random large man in the nightclub, leaning up against the bar.

The belligerent in the Hawaiian shirt nodded.

I continued as quietly as I could, "Good, his name is Leon. He likes beating the living shit out of tab skippers. Last guy went to the hospital for a week."

The man bowed up, but I saw the fear. One unintended look from the big man in our direction and a head nod from me was all it took. The brightly adorned behemoth put two twenties on the bar and left without another word.

I wiped my hands with my bar rag and walked to the lady with the green eyes boring into the side of my head.

She leaned across the bar.

"Well, you aren't winning Most Graceful Employee of the Month. What did you say to our friend in the Hawaiian shirt?"

I smile a crooked smile. "I told him the boogeyman is real, and he hates guys in Hawaiian shirts."

She quipped, "Boogeyman? Did you fail to tell him about the boogeywoman? It's 2023 after all."

I laughed genuinely. *First one of those tonight*, I thought to myself.

"What can I get for you, ma'am?"

A perfectly manicured eyebrow lifted, and a devilish smile split her face.

I felt a shudder run through me. It was as if she could see through me.

"Double Johnnie Walker black, with one ounce of mineral water, please."

"I don't think I have ever made one of those."

Her smile shifted and touched her eyes. Her hands were clasped together as if in prayer. Her shoulders slumped, making her look smaller than she really was.

I quickly poured eight seconds worth of whiskey into a snifter and then poured Perrier water into the glass.

"Would you like to start a tab?" I asked in my practiced customer-service timber.

She slid a credit card to me. I took the card and walked to the register. The black American Express said, *Arrangements by Ariel.* I made a conscious effort to not comment on the rare sight. I started the tab and handed her the card back.

Her full smile was gone. Nothing but focus lived in those glowing eyes, and she was not focused on me. The large man in the Hawaiian shirt was back near the bar. She moved through the throng and ended up right next to him. She brushed past him. Her hand drifted casually over his drink, and I must have been mistaken, but she opened her hand and let something go.

She walked to the dance floor and disappeared.

"Sammi. SAMMI!" B-Don yelled at me from halfway down the bar. "I need three Brain Hemorrhages and one White Russian."

I snaped back into my rhythm. The interesting woman and large, flower-adorned man forgotten. I shook the White Russians, layered the Brain Hemorrhages, and the rhythm took me back into the flow of the bar.

The Seattle nightlife spun and jumped to the beat of the music, quieting the voices of self-doubt that flowed through me not an hour ago. I understood the draw of nights like this. It's the suspension of consequences that draws the crowd. The removal of future and past is the main intoxicant while the alcohol and drugs were close seconds.

The moments turned to hours, and finally, B-Don Signaled the DJ, and shouts of last call started echoing through the club. The rush of people to the bar was overwhelming.

I slung drinks with the rest of my team to the screams of the crowd. The bouncers started moving through the crowd, encouraging the patrons to leave. I closed out check after check. The crowd grew smaller and smaller.

A voice cut through the receding deluge of sound. "I think I need to pay you."

I turned to see the black-haired woman and those luminescent green eyes staring at me. Her entire demeanor spoke of a quiet confidence. Her fingernails were plain, which, while not unusual, certainly clashed with the frightfully colorful deluge of humanity beside and behind her.

I nodded my head, saying, "You could run for it, but I do have your card info."

She shrugged. "How would you get your tip then?"

I shrugged back. "I guess I would have to chase you, but I don't like your odds in those heels. What did you put into our floral friend's drink?"

Her demeanor shifted from flirty and confident to colder than ice in less than a millisecond.

"What?" she reacted, her eyes appraising me as if for the first time.

I asked again, "What did you slip into the big guy's drink?"

She shook her head and spoke, "The only thing in his drink is what he paid for."

I let it go, making no further comment. She took the receipt and left a perfectly average tip of 20 percent. I barely saw her black hair sway as she stepped out the front door into the gray Seattle night.

The last of the customers shuffled out. The other bartenders and I sat down and began to count the evening's take.

B-Don let his persona slip, and Brendon Wheeler joined us as the bartender gave way to the middle-age, lovable stoner. He lit an American Spirit ultra light with his Zippo. He took a deep drag off it and leaned back in his seat.

"Well, buddy, that's another one in the books. How did we do, Joe?"

Joe was a portly gentleman who had a devil-may-care attitude about everything, especially customers.

"Not bad, three hundred apiece. Not that you bitches deserve any of it." Pointing at himself, he remarked, "Talent." Pointing back at us, he said, "Support."

Joe handed money to Brendon, who took his cut and handed me my cut for the evening.

I shook his hand and said, "Thank you, brother," instilling as much feeling as I could into the statement.

His name may be Brendon, but the only reason I knew that was because of Facebook. I had only ever called him B-Don.

Three months ago, I met B-don walking down the street near Ox's Pool Hall in Downtown Seattle. I was lying to some suit in the street, trying to get a handout.

B-Don stopped and said, "Hey, man, do you have a job?"

"Not today," I replied.

With a sparkle in his eye, he replied, "Do you think you could learn to bartend?"

Lying my ass off, I instantly responded, "Absolutely."

I had never once thought of bartending, but this bearded man in the fedora presented me with something I had not received in my two years in Seattle—hope.

One month of pouring water and counting to four and many chewings-out later, I was a bartender at the Sarajevo Night Club. Returning to the moment, I pocketed my money for the evening.

B-Don asked me, "What was the deal with that nice lady with the eyes?"

"What lady?" I stammered while taking a draw of my e-cig.

B-Don's laugh echoed in the empty club. "What's wrong, buddy? You don't want to kiss and tell?"

I snorted. "Kiss? A girl? I shouldn't dare to dream."

Joe chimed back in, "I am sure if you squint hard enough, B-Don might be pretty enough for you. Alright. Night, bitches."

He put on an incredibly small pink Hello Kitty backpack and walked through the back door, with a peace sign over his head.

B-Don leaned back and exclaimed, "Shots?"

"Shots," I agreed.

B-Don slipped behind the bar and poured two shots of Jameson into plastic cups. We tapped the cups together and tapped the table before downing the whiskey. The warm liquid burned and left hints of copper pennies and sugar cookie notes as it worked its way to our livers.

B-Don asked, "Any plans for tomorrow?"

I shook my head. "Nah, I have to get Ol'bessy worked on, but then nothing for the rest of the day."

Ol'bessy was the pet name I had given to my 2004 Honda Ruckus. It was selected painstakingly from a small dealership and bought for nine hundred dollars cash, which I thought was a great deal at the time. Because I basically had no gift for mechanical things nor any idea of the value of anything that had between one and four wheels. I bought it because I was tired of walking to work, and I eventually planned on rejoining society; that meant transportation. I had already replaced most of the small scooter leading up to this conversation.

"Again?"

I nodded. "Yes, again, I think the fuel pump this time, but it could also be the flux capacitor for all I know."

"Well, as long as the hyper drive still works, you are probably good to go."

"Anyway, what are you up to?"

B-Don shrugged, adjusting his glasses and stroking his grey-white beard.

"Eh, I might smoke some weed. Okay, I am, in fact, going to smoke some weed, but Frank Turner is playing at The Showbox tomorrow night, so I will be sleeping for most of the day. If Ol'bessy is up to it, do you want to go?"

I nodded enthusiastically.

"If nothing comes up, I would love to go. How much are the tickets?"

B-Don exhaled a lungful of smoke and said plainly, "For you? Free ninety-nine."

I held my hands up in protest. "Come on, man, tell me how many doll hairs."

B-Don shook his head. "His music saved my life once upon a time and, through me, yours as well. It's my treat."

B-Don was referring to an incident a month ago, where I was at his house, sitting on his couch, talking to him about how far I had fallen, how hard I had fucked my life up, and how there was no hope. There might have been a little alcohol involved.

B-Don, in that way that only he could, screamed, "Shut the fuck up!"

He turned on Frank Turner's "Get Better" live on the TV and walked to the kitchen and returned seconds later with a black marker in his right hand and a devilish grin on his face.

The song built to the verse, and the words, "She drew a line across the middle of my broken heart and said, 'Come on now, let's fix this mess.' We could get better because we're not dead yet," played loud out of the soundbar under his TV.

Before I realized what was happening, he pounced on me, lifted my shirt, and drew a diagonal line across my chest, above where my heart was.

"You're not dead yet, which means you can get better. So build your life into something beautiful and get fucking better."

I cried, then I laughed, then we hugged, then we got super high and drunk. It was one of the greatest nights of my life.

That was the turning point for me. From that moment, I had developed into something resembling a functional human being. With hope for the future well in hand, I threw myself into bartending with reckless abandon.

I remembered the incident with fondness.

I nodded, accepting the generous offer, and said quietly, "Thank you."

B-Don smiled. "You're welcome."

— Chapter 2 —

Quid Pro Quo

I BEGAN THE FIVE-BLOCK walk to my three-bedroom, four-roommate apartment in the gray, cold, 4:00 a.m. Seattle morning. The sounds of vendors doing their morning prep bounced off the concrete. Exercise enthusiasts were taking advantage of the uncrowded streets.

As I walked, I thought of the nights where these streets were my home. The alleyways that food could be found in. The regular faces of my fellow homeless. The fear of what the night and the next day would bring. The uncertainty. The hopelessness. I had grown so much since then. I felt like I was faking all of it.

The lights cast strange amber shadows. My mind was blank as I crossed the intersection that headed north, away from the Sarajevo Night Club.

I contemplated the night's events, and in particular, the woman with the green eyes danced in my mind's eye. Her smoky voice was teasing me when a delivery van almost decided to make my bodily fluids a permanent fixture of his van's paint job.

His horn blared.

"Get the fuck out of the road, dumbass." His fever-pitch scream pierced the air.

I looked up and saw a green light.

I raised my hand, saying, "My bad."

I began to shuffle off, feeling embarrassed.

I looked down the street at the coffee shops and restaurants and saw two old men sitting and playing chess. I smiled and nodded to them, and they offered me a little wave in return.

My cell phone buzzed in my pocket, and an ambulance screamed by. This was so common in Seattle as to barely be of notice. I looked at my phone, and the caller ID said, *Restricted*. I answered it.

"Good morning, Samuel," a smooth female voice said.

The only one that called me Samuel was my mother, and I didn't think I was getting a call from the great beyond.

"Hi…" I stammered.

"The drink you made for me is called the Christopher Hitchens."

There was no way she got my number from someone at the bar.

"How did you get my number?"

She laughed. "Oh, I just asked someone. They were more than happy to give it to me. Do you remember what you asked me before I left?"

The hair on the back of my neck stood on end, and cortisol began to flood my body with equal parts embarrassment and fear.

"Ye—"

"Good," she stated before the S got out of my mouth.

"I am going to need you to do me a favor, and if you do, I will do one for you in the future."

Confusion and curiosity set sail in my mind.

"Okay, shoot."

"I need you to forget that I was in your bar last night, and most importantly, I need you to forget what you saw me do last night. If you do this for me, I will give you a number that you can call for one favor."

I was surprised, but I knew better than to stick my nose into other people's business.

"Okay, what kind of favor do I get?"

"You know in the game Monopoly, when you have a get-out-of-jail-free card. This is more like a get-out-of-the-ninth-circle-of-hell card. When you are in the worst spot of your life, when all seems lost and there is no way through, call that number, and whatever it is that is vexing you will just float away. Sound like a decent trade?"

Being an idiot, I said, "What if I wanted to take you to dinner?"

She laughed. "I think you may not enjoy my company as much as you think you might. But seeing as it was a joke, I'll simply add that if that is what you wanted your favor to be, I would gladly have dinner with you."

I smiled and said, "It was only a joke if you aren't interested."

This time, she laughed, full and without reservation. "Maybe one day, many miles down the road. Will you keep my secret, Mr. Howard?"

She knew my last name. That was shocking.

"I will, Ariel."

She said nothing for a long moment.

"Thank you."

Then the phone call ended. A second later, my phone buzzed, and a phone number came through in a text message. I saved the number under the name Break Glass in Case of Hell / Take Ariel to Dinner.

To my credit, she was one of the most striking people that I had ever met, so I didn't think I could be blamed for how easily I agreed to lie for her. Also, anything she did to that guy he probably deserved. I've had girlfriends, but none that hit me as hard in the chest as this one small interaction.

I thought to myself, *The healthiest thing you can do is to let go of this night and the green-eyed lady, pretend like none of it was real, and go back to the life that you are trying to build for yourself.*

But I knew in my gut, that elusive pit at the bottom of my consciousness, that this was not possible.

I made it to the apartment and punched my code in to unlock the front door. I made my way up the stairs on autopilot, deep in thought.

I considered the night I had and thought, *Well, at worst, it will make an interesting story one day.*

My key and my Snoopy key chain rattled quietly as I slid the key into the lock and entered what was affectionately dubbed by its residents the frat house.

Morning came far too early as I awoke at the crack of noon. This was the normal time for a responsible bartender to be awake. The rest of the frat house was up and going about their Sunday rituals. A game of beer-laced Madden was taking place between Alistair and Mike

I said hello, and Mike said, "Good morning to the gentleman of the night."

"Playing as the Bucs again? Do you plan on making poor Alistair play life on hard mode every Sunday?"

Mike yawned. "Sorry, couldn't hear you over the scoreboard."

I shook my head, smiling. I walked to the kitchen to begin my day with something resembling food. I settled on toast and black coffee mostly because I just didn't feel like doing anything else. My phone rang, and I saw Joe's number pop up.

"Good morning, sexy," I said.

The playful tone that was always normally in Joe's voice at times and all places was replaced by his business voice. "I need you to put clothes on and come to the bar as soon as you can."

Confused and half asleep, I stammered, "Okay, is everything alright?"

Joe said, "Yeah…but I need you down here as soon as you can."

I nodded. I felt dumb for nodding because I was on a phone. "I'll be there in an hour and a half."

"See you soon." The phone disconnected.

I ate my toast and drank my coffee in a hurry. Because if I was going to make it to the concert tonight, I had to go by Fat Cat Moto to get my scooter.

I ordered an Uber off my phone and cringed at the price. Apparently, it was peak hours, and my normal eighteen dollars to get to Fat Cat's was replaced by thirty-five dollars. I was not overly money conscious because of my new well-paying job. I had more money than I ever had my entire life. It still bothered me.

Fifteen minutes later, I took my Uber to Fat Cat's, and I walked inside to see Walter. Walter looked like his hands had been permanently stained black from years of turning wrenches.

"Hey there, Sammi. Good to see you again."

I shook his hand, not caring about the grease "I bet it is. At this rate, I am starting to feel like your retirement plan."

He laughed. "Well, you wouldn't be if you dumped this piece of shit and let me put you on a real bike."

Over the course of the last month, we had many conversations about how the only real bikes in the world were built by Harley-Davidson.

"How much?" I asked.

Walter said, "Well, I had an old fuel pump in the back for this guy, so I'll do you a favor. $150."

I nodded, trying to think of a good reason to negotiate. Finding none, I pulled out two crisp hundred-dollar bills.

"I'll get you change."

Walter came back a few minutes later

"Here you go, Sammi. Please, for the love of God, don't get run over on this thing, okay? I can't afford to lose you at this point."

I shook Walter's hand again, thanking him, and I promised to see him real soon.

Walter laughed and said, "Please not too soon. I don't think I can bring myself to work on that rolling shit stick for at least a month!"

— Chapter 3 —

The Lie

I donned my helmet and began the eighteen-minute drive to Sarajevo. My scooter felt like a new machine, and I gunned the engine. Instead of a roar or the whine of a crotch rocket, my ruckus sounded like a combination between a damaged toy and a kazoo being blown by a very large clown.

The drive was mindless. As the minutes passed, I turned onto the last street before the nightclub parking area. What I saw almost dislodged me from my seat. I saw reporters gathered in front of the club and four police cars in the parking area.

I immediately began to panic as the phone call from Ariel the previous evening began to make sense. I filled in the blanks instantly. The big guy in the Hawaiian Shirt was dead. Ariel killed him, and she wanted me to cover it up for her by lying about what I saw. I made a choice. I would not give this incredibly scary woman an excuse to kill me just as efficiently as she had killed the large, angry man.

I took several deep breaths, remembering a piece of advice an old Vietnam vet had imparted to me in the homeless camp.

"Your breathing controls your calm. If you are ever in a situation that calls for calm, but you can't get calm, just, ya know, breathe in for four seconds, hold for four seconds, and exhale four seconds. Pause four seconds. Repeat."

I did this now, and it worked. In for four, hold for four, out for four. Pause for four. I felt calm as I parked my scooter and went in the club's back entrance.

Joe was standing at the bar when I walked in, talking with what was certainly a detective, while other officers and CSI personnel took pictures of the establishment.

Joe waved me over.

"Detective, this is Sammi. He was one of the bartenders that worked last night."

The detective made a note on a legal pad and then said, "Hello, Sammi, it's nice to meet you. I'm Detective Bardwell with Seattle PD. Do you know this man?"

The bald detective turned a smartphone around so that I could see the screen. It had a picture of the rude Hawaiian-shirt-wearing guy from the previous evening. I felt my heart pound in my ears. But I answered calmly and smoothly.

"Yes, he was here last night."

The detective nodded and asked, "Did you see him have any disagreements or anything that would lead you to believe that someone wanted to hurt him in any way?"

I had flashes of images moving through my mind, bass, blinding lights, Ariel, her hand drifting so innocently over the man's drink.

I shook my head.

"No, I don't think so."

The detective took out a piece of paper out of his bag and handed it to me.

"Do you know what these words here are?"

I read the paper at the spot where his thumb indicated. The words were dimethylmercury, hemotoxin, cytotoxin.

I shook my head. "I don't." The blank look on my face seemed to sell it.

"That's not too surprising. This is an unbelievably lethal cocktail of poisons. It is basically guaranteed death. Most poisons have a high-percentage chance to kill you, but something like this is as close to certainty as is humanly possible."

I nodded.

"So what happened?"

Detective Bardwell sighed. "At four fifty this morning, 911 received a call from Edward Gallo, the man in the picture I showed you. He requested an ambulance. His stated symptoms on the phone were slurred speech, drooping eyelids, and he couldn't move his leg. The ambulance crew thought it was a stroke and took him to Harborview Medical Center, where ER doctors worked on him for an hour. He was pronounced dead at six o'clock this morning. Considering the strange symptoms that at that point included arrhythmias and hemorrhages all over his body and at the insistence of his wife, who was screaming that 'someone did this to him'"—Bardwell made little air quotes—"we performed an autopsy immediately and ran a toxicology panel. Along with alcohol and cocaine, which were there in moderate levels, those three toxins were heavily present in his blood. So unless Mr. Gallo was a professional poisoner and accidently got high on his own supply, he was murdered."

I nodded and showed genuine surprise. My heart was in my throat, and adrenaline was dumping through my body. I felt sweaty.

"That's crazy."

The detective returned the nod and asked, "Did you see him talking to anyone, or did you see anyone that could have put something in his drink? Anything at all?"

This was the moment, I looked up at the ceiling as if in thought. I ignored the screaming, burning, gross sensation in my ears.

"I don't think so. There were a lot of people around him, but we could check the cameras. We have several, and he should have been in view of them most of the night."

The detective said quickly, "We already had a cursory look at those recordings, and nothing appears to be out of place. We didn't see anything on them that would lead us in a good direction."

I frowned. "Is there any chance it happened somewhere besides here? He left early in the night."

The detective nodded. "We are working those angles as well. Can I get some contact info for you in case I have any other questions?"

He handed me his pad and a pen. I carefully wrote down my address, full name, and phone number.

He smiled. "Thank you for your cooperation, Sammi. We will be in touch if anything else is needed."

The detective turned on his heel and started out the door.

Relief washed over me like a cleansing wave of water erasing footprints from a beach. I was very careful not to show my relief as I noticed another detective watching me watch Bardwell walk out the door.

Joe waited until the detectives and officers had walked out the front door.

"So did you do it?"

"You think I'm smart enough to know how to poison someone? You really are too sweet to me."

"True, but you made his last round of drinks before he went home."

"Yes, but it was three Long Islands. How would I have known which one he would take?"

"I guess your alibi is strong then. I won't call the detective to tell him you did it, I guess."

I laughed voluminously in the empty and echoey space.

"Well, thanks, Joe. It's good to have a friend like you."

He shrugged. "I am certain that you wouldn't kill him on purpose. But I have drank your Long Islands, and well. It wouldn't surprise me if they kill someone one day."

I laughed. He laughed. I gave him the middle finger, and he laughed harder. I thought to myself, *Well, you got that part right… asshole.*

I made my way to the front exit and, as an afterthought, remembered that there were reporters out there. I instead opted for the back exit.

I walked toward the open parking lot. My head swirled with conflicting thoughts and feelings—a mixture of guilt and excitement. In combination, these interwoven paradoxes led to me opening my phone and looking at the contact listed as Break Glass in Case of Hell / Take Ariel to Dinner. I thought about calling the number. I thought better of it, and instead, I googled Arrangements by Ariel.

It took me to a florist's website, but there were two different locations listed. One was an office building in Downtown Seattle. The other was a small florist shop. There were Google reviews and a phone number. 4.9 stars. Not bad. I thought again about calling the number, but I had some time before the concert tonight. I plugged the office address into my phone and started up Ol'bessy.

― Chapter 4 ―

Arrangements by Ariel

I MADE THE TURN onto seventh street, mindless to the world around me, and the Bluetooth earbuds chimed, "You have arrived."

The skyscraper loomed over me as I pulled into the ground-floor parking structure. There was a bank of elevators on the left as I pulled in. Two security guards in black suit jackets were standing there impassively.

I parked my scooter and secured the helmet to the seat. I started toward the security guards by the elevator, making sure to keep my hands neutral and by my side.

One of the two tall men stepped between me and the elevator. "Good afternoon, sir. Can I help you?"

My deer-in-the-headlights expression probably didn't help me out much.

I stammered, "I am looking for Arrangements by Ariel."

The man's face was impassive, but his guard had obviously gone up.

"What is your name?" he said sternly but not unkindly.

"Sammi."

The man spoke into a mic concealed in his sleeve. "Wait here." He pointed to a spot next to the elevator banks.

A few minutes went by. The man in the suit had not moved or made a sound.

I thought to myself, *Well, these guys must be fun at parties*.

Five minutes turned into fifteen minutes, and the man who had first spoken said, "Fifty-sixth floor. Go to the secretary's desk at the back of the lobby and give her your name."

The man reached into his pocket and handed me a guest key card.

"When the elevator door closes, you will need to scan this on the reader under the buttons."

I nodded, taking the key card. "Thanks."

I stepped into the elevator and pressed the button labeled 56. A gentle electronic voice said, "Please scan key card."

I complied.

The elevator zipped up, and blood rushed from my head for a second. Twenty seconds later, the elevator dinged, and the doors opened into a room that looked like something out of a fantasy movie. The walls were black granite, and in stark contrast, the floor was matte marble white. The front lobby was massive. There was a fountain in the middle of the room, with all manner of deer, elk, fish, and dolphins sculpted into it; and the water flowed and danced in random patterns all over the surface of the fountain. The lighting was more like an art museum than a business office.

The front desk was a giant slab of black granite with gold accents. There was a small, pale lady in her mid-forties tucked between four monitors. There were two large couches that ran along the walls beside the fountain. Next to the receptionist's desk was a full bar cart. Complete with old-fashioned glasses and martini glasses. Being a bartender, I looked at the bottles that they had on deck: Pappy Van Winkle 25 Years, a bottle that would cost me six months' worth of tips; Louis XIII Cognac; and a bottle of Cambridge Distillery Watenshi Gin, a solid five-thousand-dollar bottle of the world's most exclusive small-batch gin. This set me back a step and made me realize that this place was meant for the wealthy and powerful.

Regaining my composure, I stepped up to the desk.

"The nice man by the elevator told me to give you my name. I'm Sammi."

The woman looked up from her computer and smiled. "Ariel is expecting you. If you have a seat in the lobby, she will see you in just a few minutes."

I smiled and nodded in that canned "thank you for doing your job" sort of way. Before I stepped away, she motioned toward the bar cart.

"Can I make you a drink while you wait?"

I stopped and looked back at the best three bottles of alcohol I had ever seen with two thoughts in my head. I really wanted to taste all three of those bottles, and I didn't think Ariel would approve of me saying yes for some reason.

Why do I care what this woman thinks of me? I thought to myself. *Maybe it's because I don't feel like I deserve something that nice?*

"No, thank you."

I walked away from the desk and sat on the ridiculously comfortable couch. The leather of the couch didn't have the telltale, synthetic smell of fake leather. It smelled of polish and rawhide, a combination that relaxed me into the couch even further. If I sat here for more than a couple minutes, I would be asleep. More feelings of inadequacy flowed through my now-anxiety-filled limbs.

I looked at my clothing. A flannel shirt with red-and-white stripes, jeans that had obviously been well used, and my trusty Dr. Marten boots—well-worn and scuffed. I began to feel even more out of place. The black granite walls of the lobby made me feel like I was in a dungeon and art-deco display room that had been combined.

I noticed cameras were situated at all corners of the room. But the black backdrop made them almost invisible.

Another minute passed.

"Sammi?"

I stood and walked back to her desk, feeling like I was in a doctor's office.

"Ariel will see you now. Go down the hall and take a right until you get to the door with the big letter A on it."

I looked around like a lost puppy looking for a door to go through. The blank wall on the secretary's right lit up with a strange-looking set of scales on it. Something about it seemed familiar. The wall parted and slid open, revealing the entrance of a much-less-ornate but no less beautiful hallway, with soft jade-green accents and marble floors. Frosted glass walls ran the length of the hallway, with small placards beside every door. The lighting, which seemed to come from everywhere, was tucked into the creases at the top of the walls and by the floor.

I read the placards as I passed. Logistics, Acquisitions, Accounting, IT. I turned right, and the space between doors got much larger. The placards read, Sales Conference Room, Call Center, Lounge, Senior Analyst, Vice President, President, Senior Florist; and at the end of the hall, a massive pair of oak doors with large door knockers in the shape of the letter As made of wrought iron with silver filigree.

I stopped and looked up and down the hall. A few people were milling about when a large man came out of the lounge behind me and stepped into the door that said IT. Another man came out of the office that was marked with the placard that said Senior Florist. The man was around six feet, with a red-and-black mohawk. Tattoos covered most of his exposed flesh.

I turned back to the doors and took a breath, stepped forward, and gently knocked with the massive letter A. The door fell inward, and I almost fell in with it, as my hand was still attached to the knocker. And inside the massive room was Ariel.

— Chapter 5 —

Vidar

ARIEL WAS SITTING BEHIND an ancient-looking oak desk. She had on a Metallica T-shirt with little rips in the sleeves. Her green eyes drilled into me like spikes of ice.

In her hand was a copy of *The 48 Laws of Power* by Robert Greene. I looked around her office in wonderment. Massive bookshelves lined the walls of the office to the right. There were animal mounts from all parts of the world: a moose, an elk, grizzly bear, bull shark, nilgai, and a diorama mount behind the desk of four massive wolves.

A giant version of her necklace pendant stood above the wolves mounted to the wall. I recognized it from a World War II documentary as a Fairbairn–Sykes fighting dagger. Around the office, in small lit cases, were various weapons from different historical time periods: a gladius, a katana, an atlatl, an ancient-looking bow in a side sling quiver with handmade arrows.

As if to add juxtaposition to the strange seventy-five-year-old billionaire-style office, there were stunning flower arrangements containing red, white, and yellow roses with baby's breath, and in the middle of both arrangements, a Kadupul, which sat in the middle of the roses. Two identical flower arrangements of this sort sat at both ends of the desk.

In the middle of the desk sat a simple silver and black nameplate. Ariel Vidar Owner / CEO. She smiled warmly, and my heart fell into my shoes. The smile was nothing special, but the promise behind it was. Feeling the brief flash of lust and curiosity took me off balance for a moment. But the pressing scale of the office returned me to center. I felt like I just walked into the lair of a supervillain.

She stood and walked across the gray polished stone floor and extended her hand. I took it and was surprised by the strength of her grip.

"Welcome to our office, Sammi," she said, and motioned to one of the tufted leather chairs in front of her desk. She turned the other one slightly to face me.

She spoke first. "I am sure that you have been approached by the police, am I correct?"

"They asked for me at the club this afternoon. They asked me questions about toxins and if I saw anything unusual."

Ariel nodded. "And how did you answer them?"

"I said nothing. As agreed."

She smiled and leaned back in the chair. "So you gave him no information on me or anything that we discussed?"

"No, nothing."

"Thank you. I think you will find this might be able to help your conscience out a bit."

She walked behind her desk and picked out an envelope and walked it over and handed it to me.

I opened the envelope, and there was a giant stack of hundred-dollar bills. My eyes went wide. I had never seen so much money in my entire life.

I looked at her quizzically. "Is this my favor?"

She had a crooked smile on her angular face.

"No, that is for keeping your word to me. If we spend any additional time together in the future, you will find there is nothing I value more than that."

"How do you know I didn't lie to you?" I asked stupidly.

She giggled like she was twelve and I had just told a fart joke.

She reached into her jeans pocket and pulled a small remote out. Pushing the Play button, a screen appeared out of the ceiling, and footage from the nightclub started to play. I watched in disbelief as my conversation with Detective Bardwell played over speakers unseen.

Arrangements by Ariel

I looked at her with utter shock. "You already knew I didn't spill the beans. So why the questions?"

"First rule of interrogation, my young padawan learner: never ask an opening question to which you don't already know the answer."

I folded my arms. "Assassin, billionaire, florist, and interrogator. Is there anything that you can't do?"

She giggled with genuine warmth. "I cannot and should not sing. That's something that you have going for you."

I shook my head in wonder. "How the actual living shit fuck do you know I can sing?"

She stepped back behind her desk and pulled out a massive folder rubber-banded together and showed me the front cover. It read Samuel E. Howard. She dropped it on the desk with a dramatic thump and sat back down. She crossed her legs and made a little pyramid out of her hands.

"There is not a single thing I don't know about you, Sammi. I know where you come from. I know what your fifth-grade teacher's name was. I know what hospital you were born in. I know what your favorite color is, and I know down to an extremely accurate set of metadata what kind of porn you like. Every state-sponsored therapist you went to as a child, every transcript of the sessions, I have read all of it, and do you know what I learned?"

I shook my head, taking this in. I felt dizzy, sick, and embarrassed.

"I learned that you may be one of the only people in this country that doesn't consider themself the main character in their story. You have no ulterior motives, no ridiculously conceived ambitions or unattainable goals. Your family is all long dead. Your political positions are very-well-thought-out for someone your age. Your outlook on life went from homeless and dead by thirty-five to reasonably well-adjusted person in three months. You are looking for a purpose, and I don't think you have found it yet."

I am still and speechless. She had cut all the way to my heart, laid it open, and showed it to me.

She continued, "Do you know who that man was that I killed?"

"Edward Gallo"

She shook her head. "That's his name, but that is not who he is."

She walked back behind her desk for the third time. She took out six giant file folders much like mine, but larger. She sat back down and pointed at the folders

"Every paper in those folders details Mr. Gallo's time on terra firma. He was a corporate and political fixer. Anytime a giant company, hyper-empowered individual, or government runs into a problem for which there was no conventional solution, they would call him, and he would make the problem disappear. Just this year, Kebbi State, Nigeria, eighty civilians killed to draw out a vigilante force, and once drawn out, they were massacred. Moura Mali, three hundred civilians killed after Wagner group lifted an ISIS siege. He organized the assassination of a local leader in Cameroon and then attacked the funeral, killing thirty-two civilians—all of whom were loyal to that leader. This removed the resistance to local mining contracts in that region. My point is, our job here is to find out who is most likely to cause harm en masse and remove them from the equation. Then we study the second, third, and fourth magnitude aftereffects. For that service, we are well-paid. Oh, also we make world-class flower arrangements."

She sat back impassively after this summary. She watched my response like a hawk appraising a trout.

"I...I don't know what to say. I am not sure why you are telling me this."

She leaned forward, sighing. "Sammi, do you know what your IQ is?"

I shook my head. "Around the same level as a head of cabbage?"

She shook her head and snorted a truly ugly laugh that she just barely managed to stifle. "No, dumbass, your IQ is 149. You could literally do anything that you set your mind to. You are in the top one percentile of people on the planet."

I shook my head incredulously as I studied her face for hints of deception, as if she would tell me this was all a joke and she killed that guy because she didn't like his shirt.

"I still don't understand what you want from me."

She sighed heavier this time. "I want you to work with us. Train and become a force for good in this world. You will find no higher purpose in life than this. Trust me, I tried."

I nodded more out of being agreeable than actual assent. "I need to think about this for a while. I am not even sure what questions to ask."

She nodded. She walked from her desk and moved like she was heading toward the door. I started to stand, and an arm snaked around my neck. A sharp pain stabbed into my arm. Just as quickly as the assault began, it ended. I fell out of the chair and backpedaled from her.

"What the fuck was that?"

My backpedaling was embarrassing, but I did watch her kill someone with poison not even a day ago.

She waved a little futuristic-looking syringe.

"Just a little something to keep you safe. It will let us track you and hear what's going on around you. Because make no mistake, Sammi, you already decided to help us, and that comes with risk and danger. Whether you continue to help us is up to you, but you still could suffer some repercussions for the small part you have already played."

I stood up and regained my composure to the best of my ability. I stated flatly, "Um, I have to go to a concert."

She scrunched her face up in confusion. "Okay."

I looked back at her, feeling silly. "I am not sure why I told you that." I gave my arm a little shake.

"Yeah, I think we will be able to hear it better than you will, with the epidermis mic in the top of your tracker."

I narrowed my eyes. "What?"

"There is a very, very tiny microphone just under the top eighth millimeter of your skin that anchors there and allows us to hear the outside world out of your arm. Wait till you see the forehead camera."

I shook my head in astonishment.

Pulling the spot she had injected up next to my mouth, I said, "Testing, is this thing on?"

"Thanks, you probably just deafened the tech calibrating that thing."

I said quietly toward the spot on my arm, "Sorry."

She smiled, and it touched the corners of her eyes, which showed small lines at the corners.

Maybe she is older than I think she is, I thought.

I let seriousness into my voice. "Okay, I need time to think about this. Is that allowed?"

"Of course, but don't take too long to decide. You are in danger, and if life has taught me anything it is that when seconds count help is only minutes away."

I nodded and stood to leave. Ariel stood and walked with me.

"I hope you will choose to work with us. I am tired of being the only nonspecial ops or former criminal that works here. It would be nice to have a normal person around."

The question I should have asked five minutes ago finally occurred to me. "How do you choose?"

She shook her head, and then understanding crossed her face. "Follow me. I'll show you."

We walked out of the office and took a left down an identical hallway that had silver door placards that read COO, CFO, Storage, and at the end of the hall, there was a green, jade-colored wall with a small set of scales engraved into it—the kind of scales that were used in ancient times to buy and sell things.

As we got closer, I noticed that on one side of the scales, there was a heart, and on the other was a feather. A distant memory of a kid's TV-show episode that I couldn't quite place about the scales of Anubis came to my mind for a moment.

She walked up to the wall, and a seam appeared and opened into a Greek amphitheater. The room was empty. At the center of all the amphitheater were three seats and a massive screen that was suspended above them.

Ariel motioned to the large chairs on the stage.

"That is where the Norns sit when they are in their moot. Yes, they are called Norns. My great-grandfather was a little dramatic. And, yes, it is called the Norn moot. The Norns are elected from the pool of seats you see in front of you. They are the ones that decide. The person that sits in my chair can veto any decision that they make, but that has only been done twice to my knowledge in the seventy-six years we have operated."

I shook my head, imagining all the problems with this arrangement.

"Why do these people get to choose who lives and who dies? Isn't there a magic loom or some creed or other arbitrary, esoteric way to choose that is, ya know, mystical?"

She shook her head seriously.

"Everyone that is ever in this room to make choices has a background in a select group of disciplines: judges, psychologist, game theorists, philosophers, and sociologists. They are sworn to secrecy and the knowledge that if they ever told anyone how they spent their time that they would be dead before the words left their mouths."

I held my hands up, interrupting her. "Whoa, what the fuck do you mean? They would…be killed instantly?"

She smiled sadly. "Well, Sammi, this is the part that is not so warm and fuzzy. The chip in your arm serves another far-more-important function. If you begin talking about us. Or betray us in any way…" She snapped her fingers dramatically. "You're dead."

I let this thought sink in, and then the anger hit me like a wave of white-hot fire.

"Are you fucking telling me you put a death chip in my arm? What the fuck are you talking about right now? I am so fucking mad I don't even know what to say!"

Ariel made soothing motions with her hands. "Listen, I know it seems bad, but I promise you the alternative is much worse."

Ariel keyed a hidden earpiece. "Skuld, play the proliferation video."

A short clip played on the massive screen. It showed a time line, starting with the creation of the atomic bomb up to now. Ariel explained as the animated graph started to trend upward.

"Here is why…well…one of the whys anyway."

The graph showed the number of ways that humanity could destroy itself. The number of actual methods that existed and the number of people that had access to those methods. The number became massive when the graph reached 2023. I wasn't exactly calm, but this did have a sobering effect.

Ariel stepped from my side and pointed up at the large screen.

"This is how the world ends. But it isn't the only problem we have."

She motioned me out of the large auditorium.

"We will have way more time to talk about that sort of thing once you decide to join us." Her foxlike grin came so easy, and she seemed so confident in what she was saying.

"I need to go. B-Don is going to kill me if I am late to this concert."

"Frank Turner, right? It's going to be a hell of a show."

I shook my head. "Stop doing that. I need at least the illusion of privacy. Also, how did you go from not knowing I was going to a concert to knowing which one?"

She snorted. "I am sure some of the people that sit in this room would love to debate you on whether anyone has the right to privacy. As to your second question." She pointed to her ear.

Ariel reached in her pocket and handed me a small, round disk that looked like a battery.

"If you are in a bad spot and can't call out or get to your phone, click this three times. It will make it more likely we can help you by decreasing our response time."

I nodded and slipped it into my left pocket.

"I really like B-Don. Is he as pure a soul as he appears?"

I cracked a smile. "Way purer than that."

I walked to the door, and the guy with the mohawk was waiting out in the hallway.

Ariel stepped past me. "Sammi, this is Doc. Doc, Sammi. Doc is my number two and head of operations."

I shook his hand, noticing the stripes of red that went down the side of his black mohawk and the Norse rune tattoos on his scalp and ravens on each side of his head.

I hesitantly said, "Ru-fi-o?"

His eyes lit up, and his smile was beaming. "Can't fight, can't fly, can't crow, you aren't a pan man. I am so happy you get the *Hook* reference. I think we just became best friends."

I smiled and tried to wrap my head around the certainly badass man in front of me having a nerd moment.

"Well, apparently, if I say yes to Ariel's offer here, I may learn to do one of those things."

He nodded. "Yeah, and I will probably be one of your instructors, but there will be no invisible food fights. At least I don't think there will be."

I laughed, Ariel looked lost, and we both looked at her in dumbfounded disbelief.

"Wait a second," I said.

Doc's mouth opened in utter shock. "There is no fucking way that you... Holy shit."

Ariel put her hands up in surrender and started backing away from this situation that she had accidentally helped make. Her sudden vulnerability was endearing.

Doc and I blurted out at the same time, "You haven't seen *Hook*!"

"This is an injustice," I stated flatly. "An outrage."

Doc played along. "Is there a government agency I can call to report your friends and loved ones for not showing you, nay, forcing you to watch that masterpiece?"

She was half laughing along, half not understanding.

"I can't join you. Not until you watch *Hook*. I refuse to have a boss that does not understand the source of joy that is that movie."

"I am requesting a leave of absence, Vidar," Doc said.

She looked stunned and responded sharply, "For fucking why?"

Doc continued mournfully, "Well, until you watch *Hook*, I am afraid that your moral compass could not possibly be centered enough to do this job effectively."

She shook her head in disbelief. "Okay, okay, I am out of here in about an hour. I will go home immediately and watch *Hook*. Is that solution agreeable to all present?"

Doc nodded and said, "I expect one reference a day after you watch it for at least three months, or I won't believe you."

I nodded and said, "Until such time, as I am also convinced of the truth of your claim, I cannot join."

She shook her head. "A business valued at just over a billion dollars and a black budget slush fund from the US government and other allied governments around eight billion dollars a year, and I am sitting here, being berated about not seeing a summer blockbuster from 1990 that probably isn't even an hour and a half long. At least you aren't trying to make me watch *Lord of the Rings* extended editions."

Me and Doc were obviously shocked.

"Actually, it came out in ninety-one," I started.

Doc finished, "And its run time is two hours and fifteen minutes."

Ariel shook her head and said, "I can't decide whether to unalive both of you or myself."

Ariel and Doc both walked me to the elevator in relative silence.

As we came to the elevator, I stopped like I had been frozen solid. All at once, I realized that the entire world that I used to view as uncomplicated was now a much-scarier place. A place where there were unknown monsters around every corner, and some of them wanted me for dinner. It was fear that held my feet to the ground. As if they had been Gorilla Glued to the polished marble, I stood motionless as the illusion of the world I had lived in crashed down around my ears like a building falling on me.

I realized that I had been standing silently for at least a minute or two. Ariel and Doc both waited for me patiently.

"It's okay, buddy. The first time you realize someone wants you dead is the hardest. It is a weird and uncomfortable feeling, but you get used to it. But don't forget this, complacency kills," Doc said.

I nodded. "Thanks."

Ariel stuck her hand out, and I shook it. "Be seeing you, Sammi," she said with a bewitching smile, and then the elevator doors slid closed.

— *Chapter 6* —

Not Dead Yet

I exited the elevator, stepping quickly past the security guards. I headed for Ol'bessy. I popped on my helmet and started her up.

I turned on some blues in my Bluetooth earbuds. When I checked the time, I saw that it was almost 6:30 p.m. About time for me to head over to B-Don's house for the concert.

Putting his address into my phone, my mind began to wander back through the conversation with Ariel. There was so much about the conversation that felt unreal.

The secret cabal of noble assassins that did what? Killed people that they thought would become a problem? Ariel's smile returned unbidden to the forefront of my mind. Doc's easygoing nature. The impossibility of it. Thoughts, random, and unorganized rained in my consciousness like motes of dust caught in sunlight. I reminded myself what I just learned was real and not some dreamed-up video-game setting.

What was the criteria? Did their targets have to kill people before getting on the moot's list? Like Dexter? Or did they just have to make a bad social-media post?

Too many questions overwhelmed my brain at the same time, and I eventually just became numb to the idea. Like electricity and oxygen, it became in my mind part of reality.

As I wound my way out of the parking garage, a memory of my father when I was young replayed itself unasked.

"Son, try not to bite off more than you can chew. Life ain't about what you do for you. But if you don't take care of you, you can't take care of anyone else. And taking care of others is all that matters."

I felt the welling of tears tug at the corner of my eyes.

I lost myself in the drive and started to feel a little better about now having a death chip in my arm.

I rationalized, "Everyone dies. There is nothing different now than when I woke up today."

Another question sang its testing song. "Who the fuck are they to decide who lives and dies?"

I answered that one for myself immediately. "They are they, the ones in the darkness that made life and death their only discipline. In a way, those are the only kinds of people that can decide."

I pulled into B-Don's driveway and saw the Thunder Chicken parked and gleaming in the sunlight. B-Don's baby was a 1967 Ford Thunderbird Landau model, so it was half muscle car, half sedan. I had loved this car since the first time I laid eyes on her. A small sticker was on the back window of a chicken with lightning bolts in its hands.

B-Don was sitting on his front stoop, smoking a cigarette and drinking an IPA.

I parked my scooter on the side of the house and walked up to B-Don, who was wearing a Frank Turner T-shirt that said, "Not Dead Yet," in black text down the front of it.

"Hey there, good-lookin', can I take you for a ride?"

I shrugged. "Twenty dollars is twenty dollars."

B-Don smiled broadly. "And it always will be. Looks like Ol'bessy is running good. Walter hook you up?"

I smiled, shaking my head. "I am pretty sure Walter's entire financial strategy at this point is just waiting for Ol'bessy to die so he can make ends meet."

B-Don ashed his cigarette and handed a beer to me that he was concealing behind his back.

I cracked it and tapped it against his. "Cheers, brother."

We drank, and then we drank some more.

B-Don sighed and put out his cigarette. "Alright, let's ride."

I stood. "Do you mind if I leave my bag inside?"

He nodded and said, "Yeah, throw it on the couch."

I stepped inside and pulled three hundred dollars out of the envelope. I tucked it back in the bag and stepped back outside.

B-Don handed me an edible and I asked, "What's the dosage?"

"Ten milligrams."

I nodded and took it, threw it in my mouth, chewed, and swallowed.

B-Don sat down in the Thunder Chicken, and the engine roared to life. I smiled and got in the passenger seat. He turned on music for a sushi restaurant by Harry Styles and turned the volume up.

He backed out of the driveway, pulling a flask from an unknown location. He took a swig and handed it to me. I took a swig and immediately recognized the Jameson Stout edition. I nodded in appreciation and handed the flask back.

We began the twenty-minute drive from Belltown to The Showbox. The music bumped, and my head nodded to the funky bassline. As we drove and jammed out to the weird-as-fuck song that we both loved so much, I noticed there was a large Suburban that had been behind us since we left B-Don's house.

I refused to let my conversation with Ariel earlier make me paranoid, and focused my attention back on the road in front of us and the music.

Then Doc's words returned to me, "Complacency kills."

We arrived at The Showbox an hour before the show was scheduled to start. We stepped into line with all the other fans, who were obviously just as drunk and high as we were. We stepped up to the security gate, and the ticket taker scanned B-Don's phone twice. We walked up to the metal detector.

B-Don stepped through, and the machine beeped. The guard off to the right with a wand waved it over him, and it beeped on his belt buckle and nowhere else. The guard waved him through.

Then they waved me forward. I went through, and the machine beeped. I stepped off to the right the same way B-Don had, and the guard waved it over my arms, and the little wand gave the tiniest of squeaks when it passed over the location where Ariel had unceremoniously jabbed my arm with the death chip.

This immediately reminded me of the previous half of my day. Ariel's voice slipped into my mind.

"Be a force for good."

We went into the venue and got a beer and then to the merch line, where I bought the tour shirt.

The edible had started to hit me at this point, and my head was swimming as we went into the concert venue.

My mind went unasked to sad memories. I couldn't stand the idea of letting the ideal of my father down. I didn't get to have him for long, but the few memories of him I had tell me he was a good man that I should try to make proud. Would becoming a killer for the ideal of "good" make him proud?

"Shots?" B-Don asked.

I nodded. "Shots."

As we walked to the bar, B-Don asked, "You okay, buddy? You haven't said a word since we got here."

I nodded in my buzzed state. "Yeah, you got called to the bar at some point today, I assume?"

"I did. Apparently, that guy in the Hawaiian shirt last night got murdered."

"I was just thinking about that. But the guy probably deserved it."

I started kicking myself mentally before the words even finished leaving my mouth. STUPID, I thought.

B-Don looked at me in surprise. "What the fuck, man?"

"Sorry, I mean that he was an asshole. So I just don't feel that bad."

B-Don nodded.

I thought to myself quietly like B-Don could hear my thoughts, *Holy shit, that was close.*

As we arrived at the bar, B-Don said to the cute bartender, "Two Jamesons, please, neat."

She nodded, grabbed two plastic shot glasses, and poured.

We both threw a twenty on the bar, and her eyes lit up and said, "Thanks, boys. Come back and see me."

We smiled back, and B-Don said, "To not being dead yet."

My mind went back to a giant-animal-mount-covered office with a mysterious woman jabbing my arm with a needle.

"Cheers."

I smiled, and we clicked the plastic cups together then taped them on the bar as we downed the beverage. The shot burned as it went down. I could not taste it, with all the distractions that were in my head.

As the minutes passed, all the chemical-assisted endorphins that were flowing through my mind gave me a clarity of thought that I had not had before.

My brain, with its ever-present singsong soliloquy helped by explaining it to me, *Helping cover up that murder is the same as murder on an ethical level. You are not better than Ariel or any of the other people there. The fact that they see something in you being the incredible, edible dumbass that you are is nothing short of a miracle akin to Christ walking on water. If you don't take their offer, you are the biggest dumb dummy that has ever dumbed.*

I quietly told my brain to fuck off and went into the pit.

The lights came on about twenty minutes later, and the shit show began. Frank pumped the crowd up, and everyone began jumping, dancing and singing along with the music.

The concert was incredible. I was lost in the music, with the edible and alcohol coursing through me and the adrenaline of being in such a large crowd.

The last song started, and B-Don and I were smiling at each other knowingly. The song "Get Better" started, and the crowd was singing along loudly.

Fortunately, my alcohol and weed-induced state started to wane. And the words of the song I knew so well drilled into me, reminding me of all the wonderful things that had happened for me in the last three months.

The crowd roared. "With the road rising up to meet me and my enemies defeated in the mirror behind."

My road had a split in the middle of it. One way led to a normal life that might or might not be filled with joy and happiness.

The other road led to an extraordinary life with great challenges and possibly great tragedies. But a life where maybe I, the ordinary and boring person that I was, could make a difference and leave something useful behind me.

Maybe see a few enemies of my own defeated in the mirror behind.

The song started winding down, and some of the crowd began leaving.

I leaned over and asked B-Don, "Are we heading out after this song?"

B-Don shook his head. "No. Frank comes out for drinks with the crowd for a while after."

I smiled broadly and listened to the song end. He said, "Thank you very much, Seattle. Be seeing you in a minute once I get a fresh shirt on."

Everyone in the crowd laughed at that. The man looked like he had been in a dunk tank. The last notes faded, and the crowd rushed the bar.

B-Don and I stood in the giant circle that was forming around Frank and his bandmates at the bar, and eventually, we were right in front of the man himself.

We shook his hand, and one of the bandmates took a picture for us, and before we walked away, I said to Frank, "The song 'Get Better' saved my life. Thank you."

Frank had a knowing smile on his face, and he simply, quietly said, "Me too."

— *Chapter 7* —

Black Marker

WE SAID GOODBYE TO Frank. B-Don shook his hand, and Frank smiled sadly in my direction.

I smiled back.

We started walking toward the exit. The crowd had thinned out to about twenty people left in the venue. The stagehands descended on the equipment, beginning the well-rehearsed act of tearing down the set. B-Don motioned me toward the exit.

"That was an amazing show."

B-Don nodded and lit an American Spirit, offering it to me. I nodded and took it. He lit another one for himself.

B-Don smiled as he inhaled. "You know, I love you, buddy."

"I know."

B-Don laughed. "Did you just Han Solo me?

"You are far prettier than I am. You can pull off Princess Leia much easier."

He smiled a wide and sardonic smile. "Yes, I agree. You are ugly."

We walked out the front of the venue and moved briskly toward B-Don's Thunder Chicken.

As we made it to the car, I noticed immediately something was wrong, and I couldn't quite put my finger on exactly what was bothering me.

Two Sprinter vans pulled up, screeching tires and bright lights. One on the street and one at the back of B-Don's car.

The van's sliding doors opened, and three men jumped out, each with yellow shotguns in their hands. The last thing I heard before my body locked up and plummeted toward the pavement was explosions. A sound like a Wookie in heat escaped my mouth.

Before I could form a coherent thought, my hands were zip-tied around my back, and then my mouth was stuffed full of something. I heard duct tape rip off its spool, and the pressure in my mouth increased. I gagged, then my world went black.

A hood had been put over my head. I felt zip ties go around my legs, and then four strong hands picked me up and unceremoniously tossed me forward and down. I knew that I had just been dropped into the back compartment of one of the Sprinter vans.

We drove for what felt like an eternity. B-Don was beside me in the van. I could feel one of his boots against my leg. After what felt like an hour, the van stopped.

I heard doors open and then close. I heard footsteps outside the vehicle. I heard B-Don mumble something through his gag. The doors that were at my feet opened, and hands grabbed my legs and pulled me toward the exit. When I was halfway out, someone snipped the zip ties around my ankles.

Then they dragged us the rest of the way out. Firm hands gripped my arms painfully. They forced me down hard in what felt like a metal chair. I heard another chair get dragged across a concrete floor.

Another person was forced into the other chair, presumably B-Don. Without ceremony, the hood was removed, and light blinded me.

My eyes took several seconds to adjust to the overhead fluorescent lights. When I could finally see, I saw B-Don to my left. And silhouetted behind a massive floodlight was a lone figure.

A man walked out of the light, and the room came into focus. We were inside of what looked like a warehouse. The man looked at ease and moved with the smooth stride of a predator.

He slid his glasses off and tucked them in the pocket of his blue suit jacket. He slid the jacket off and folded it over an arm, revealing a leather shoulder holster. He walked over to the wall and grabbed another chair, dragging and making a production of flipping the chair around and sitting, folding his arms on the back of the chair. He didn't look at B-Don; his gray eyes bored into mine.

He lit a small cigar with a blowtorch and then said, "Hello, Sami. Before your pretty little head starts to do too much thinking, my name and who I am here representing is irrelevant. The only thing you must tell me for your friend B-Don here to go free is to tell me who killed Edward Gallo. I know you know who did it. Let's save both of us a lot of time and pain. Just nod your head if you are willing to tell me, and you can both go home."

He looked at me questioningly. I remained still, not nodding or shaking my head.

He said quietly, "If you remain silent, I will interpret it as resistance. If you resist me, I will not hurt you. Oh no… I will hurt your friend. You are going to get three chances."

He took a black marker and a pair of trauma shears. He deftly cut B-Don's pant legs off six inches above the knee. He pulled the cap off the marker and drew an X on B-Don's shin. He then drew an X above B-Don's right knee. He then grabbed B-Don's face, kissed him on the forehead, then drew an X right in the middle of B-Don's forehead. I started struggling against the restraints. B-Don did the same thing.

The mystery man put his hands out in a calming gesture.

"Let's not get crazy now. I have a gift for you and your friend."

His hand went into a pocket and pulled out two pieces of paper and a debit card. My mind was fighting with itself. If I told him anything, I would die, and then he would probably kill B-Don anyway. If I didn't tell him anything, he'd kill B-Don and then me anyway. Not seeing a way out, I set my mind to not tell him anything. Because functionally, I mused, *We are both dead. If I give him what he wants, we are dead. If I refuse, we are dead. Don't help this cunt.*

I thought about the little beacon in my pocket and tried reaching for it, but I could not move enough.

The man continued his monologue, a small whisp of smoke coming from his tiny cigarillo.

"These are two plane tickets to Peru. And this"—he waved the debit card—"is a card to an untraceable account with three hundred thousand dollars in it. That is enough for you to live quite comfortably in your new home."

He reached for the shoulder holster and retrieved a very shiny chrome 1911 handgun with engravings on the slide.

"Now, nod if you understand me. I am going to ask you the question again. If you do anything besides nod your agreement to tell me, I will start with his shin, and we will repeat this process until your friend has a nice .45 Caliber hole in his forehead."

He pointed the gun at B-Don, and I began to sputter curses through my gag. The man with the gun looked me in the eye and smiled he said, "Who killed Edward Gallo?"

I stared daggers into him.

He shook his head, sighing, and said simply, "Okay."

The small explosion in the indoor space was deafening. My ears stopped working for a second, and then sound was replaced by a ringing and muffled screaming to my left that sounded far away through the ringing in my ears.

The room was filled with smoke and dust from the ceiling, and then I made eye contact with B-Don. Surprise, pain, and fear were plastered on his face like a Halloween mask.

Tears welled up in my eyes as I saw the wound—a small hole in his shin, but the back of his calf looked like it had been put through a blender.

The guy with the gun screamed in my face, his spittle adding to the tears.

"This could have all been avoided. You could have chosen to be cooperative, but you decided your life was worth more than his."

He looked at B-Don and again pointed his 1911.

"Now, who the fuck killed Edward Gallo?"

He walked over and took off B-Don's gag with one smooth motion. B-Don was still screaming.

"Tell him, Sammi. Tell him. It doesn't matter, man. Just tell him, and we can go to the hospital. Fuck you!" He screamed at his tormentor.

I looked on, tears running freely and bile threatening to come out my nose.

Arrangements by Ariel

The man eyed me and raised an eyebrow. I stared at him hard, ripping at my restraints. The man shrugged and fired.

B-Dons screams filled my ears faster this time as the bullet struck his thigh. Blood sprayed from the new wound and slowed to a steady flow.

The man said, "Last chance, who killed—"

A boom filled the room, and gunfire could be heard from across the warehouse. A man wielding a rifle ran to the side of the guy in the blue suit and said something in his ear. They both took off, running off to my right.

B-Don groaned. "Fuck, this hurts."

I couldn't speak, but I made reassuring noises through my gag.

B-Don's exhalations turned to quite moans. Making noises through my gag, I was helpless to do anything.

He slurred something before passing out, and I threw myself in my chair, trying like hell to get out of the restraints. I felt the zip ties rip into my wrists. I flopped the chair over and tried to wriggle myself free. I felt something warm on my hands as I yanked at the plastic restraints.

Nothing was working. The minutes ticked by, and they felt like hours.

I heard more gunshots closer this time. I then heard footsteps, quite across the concrete floor. In my daze, I saw the floodlight turn off, and five figures became visible to me. All of them wore some strange Star Wars–looking helmet-mask combo.

They moved like dancers, stepping smoothly to music only they heard.

They were obviously communicating. One pointed to B-Don slumped in his chair, with a pool of blood under him. The figure in front undid an unseen seal and pulled off the helmet. A black ponytail came out of the helmet first.

And then Ariel's green eyes were locked on mine.

"You are going to be fine."

She pulled a knife from her armor and deftly sliced the zip ties off my arms and legs. I staggered to my feet and walked over to B-Don.

The other guy who I suspected was Doc started an IV, had B-Don's leg wrapped with something, and was doing chest compressions. I removed my gag and began quietly hoping for a miracle. I didn't believe in a higher power, but I was mentally screaming to the heavens.

"Please, if there is anyone up there, please save him. You good-for-nothing, worthless, sky daddy, fuck, do something!"

After about three minutes, the guy said in an electronic voice, "I'm so sorry, man. There was nothing I could do. He lost too much blood."

My head swam with pain and sadness. The hope I held so tight died in me as B-Don's corpse laid motionless. I screamed internally, letting sorrow fill me. My mind rationalized, *If I would have talked, I am certain we would both be dead anyway.*

Ariel put a kind arm around me and led me from the room.

My pain and sadness started to turn into something darker, something that, up until this point in life, I had not understood. For the first time in my life, I felt true, seething, red-hot hate.

Ariel walked me through the building. I saw a door across the way that had obviously been blown off its hinges. I saw three figures laying on the ground in pools of blood, with their hands zip-tied behind their back. Ariel passed me by the arm to one of the other nameless men in the Mandalorian-looking masks.

I passed through the blown-out door, and outside two Suburbans were sitting, waiting for us. People in the same masks that Ariel and Doc were wearing milled around and motioned us into the Suburban.

I slid in and looked back toward the building. I saw one of the men carrying a body bag draped over his shoulders. Ariel slipped into the seat next to me and slowly closed the door. Her helmet was back on, and she made a little circle in the air with her pointer finger. The Suburban leapt forward, and she slid off her helmet.

She reached over and grabbed my hand and held it. She didn't say a word, and soundlessly I began to cry.

She rubbed my hand. "We have footage of the guy who did this. When you are ready, we will balance the scales."

The look in her eyes was so reassuring I almost felt better.

I finally managed words. "How long?"

"Hard to say. It will not be easy, but when your training is done, then we will strike, together."

"What's first?"

"First, you mourn your friend, attend his funeral, and then after that, you are going to move into one of our barracks. B-Don's cause of death will be a car crash. The scene is already being set up now by some of the Azrael. Once that is done, family and friends will be alerted by authorities, and all of this"—she pointed backward—"will be like it never happened."

This made me angrier for some reason.

"So what? B-Don's death gets faked, and everyone involved gets away?"

"Oh no, no, they're not going to get away. I will make an executive pitch to the moot. We will have an order on him."

"Who was that guy? The one that got away. The one that... killed B-Don."

She flipped down a phone that was attached to her body armor.

"His name is Marquis Zarov. He was Edward Gallo's number two and best shooter. Until today, we didn't know he was in the US. We are still trying to figure out how he got in the country without us knowing about it."

I nodded, imagining his face with a bullet hole in it; the thought filled me with indominable purpose.

"I want him dead. I want to be the one to do it," I said darkly.

Ariel nodded in understanding. "I can't promise you that. But I can promise that he will die. I hope that is good enough."

"I don't know what is good anymore."

She smiled sadly. "That's what makes this life so hard. Wondering whether what you are doing is good or bad. Let me offer you some advice. Stop being afraid of being the villain. You are going to be the villain in someone's story at some point. Just as Zarov is now yours. If you want to be strong when the time comes, abandon the need to be good."

I nodded, and said quietly, like my words might shatter the glass of the vehicle if spoken too loudly, "I don't feel anything now, nothing but hate."

Ariel responded just as quietly, "I know, I've been there. Let it be fuel. Don't let it be poison."

I nodded as the Suburban left the dark side road and pulled onto a bridge that glowed and danced with light as we headed toward the shining, gray-washed night of Downtown Seattle.

Ariel looked out the window of the SUV. Her black ponytail was in her right hand as her left held mine.

She said, "I am so proud of you for not talking. That must have been that hardest thing you have ever done."

I nodded as her thumb traced little figure eights over my hand.

"It was, but I figured if I did, I was dead, and B-Don was dead anyway."

She nodded firmly. "You are right. But to act on that information in the moment." She shook her head in wonderment and said, "Bangarang."

This made me smile involuntarily, and a bitter laugh escaped my mouth before I could stifle it. Her musical laugh answered in response. I immediately felt a bit better.

She said, "Yeah, I keep my promises."

"I don't think I can go home."

She handed me a key card like the one the security guy by the elevator had given to me.

"There are apartments at the tower, one floor under my office, for occasions such as this."

I took the key card and asked, "Can I ever go home again?"

She shook her head. "No, and your roommates are currently being moved to another apartment in your building. As soon as we got word on your situation, they were removed because of a gas leak that we faked. The property owner was paid well to move them tomorrow morning into something more permanent."

I nodded. "I need to put my two weeks in at the club."

She said, "Yes. We need you to exit your current life in the most normal manner possible. But we can talk about all of that tomorrow. Tonight you need a shower, a shot, and some sleep."

I slipped my hand away from hers and noticed the blood there for the first time. She pulled a pack of baby wipes from the seat pocket in front of her and carefully cleaned the blood off my hand. She was tender as she slowly removed the stain.

"Thank you."

Her lips pulled into a small, sad smile. "You're welcome."

The Suburbans sped down the street at a breakneck pace. After another ten minutes of driving, we arrived at the building where Ariel and I had spoken last. It felt like years had passed even though it was only hours. As the Suburbans pulled into the underground parking structure, a blank concrete wall slid open and exposed a ramp that led deeper underground.

The Suburbans rolled down the ramp, the sound of their engines reflecting off the concrete walls. LED lights flicked on and lit the tunnel with a strange blue glow. It felt like we were descending for an eternity when, finally, they came to a wide-open antechamber.

The large concrete cube of a room housed several Suburbans of the same style that we were currently in. The Suburbans pulled into parking places, and all the men and women, with their helmets and rifles, began dismounting from their vehicles.

Ariel said, "This is our stop."

I grabbed the handle on the door and pushed. The door was much heavier than it appeared. The people in the masks began doing their jobs. I couldn't quite tell what exactly they were doing. All of them appeared to be communicating.

Ariel slid out of the SUV with the grace of a jaguar and began walking toward a bank of elevators.

I followed close behind. Ariel pressed the button, and a smooth stainless-steel door slid open. We both stepped into the elevator. Ariel stepped to the control panel, pressing the button for floor 56. An electronic female voice sounded from the roof of the elevator and said, "Please scan key card." Ariel placed her key card underneath the scanner, and it made a small beeping sound.

The elevator started flying upward at an incredible pace, and in my current state, it made all the blood rush from my head, and stars danced in my eyes.

Ariel pulled off her gloves. "Wanna come to my office for a drink?"

I looked at my injured wrists and though how small a thing they were. "Yeah, I think that would be appropriate."

The elevator door slid open, and we moved quickly down the hallway to Ariel's office. Ariel slid an old-looking key into the large, oaken doors. She turned the key, and a sharp click reverberated through the ancient wood. The doors soundlessly slid open.

We walked across the polished granite, and Ariel began taking off her armor one piece at a time. She sat her helmet on her desk. Pulling open the bottom drawer, her hand returned with a bottle of Ardbeg 1975.

I let out a low whistle. "What percentage of Arrangements by Ariel's budget is consumed by your ridiculously expensive alcohol selection?"

"When you spend enough time with the Norns, you get spoiled."

She pulled the cork with the telltale slipping and popping sound of a bottle that had not been opened in some time. She poured an indeterminate amount of the pale-yellow liquid into highball glasses.

The smell of smoke hit my nose before she handed me the glass. She held out the cool crystal highball glass, and I took it. Taking in the sweet, smoky, medicinal notes of the whiskey, I let the burning smell hit my sinuses.

I took a very small sip and was surprised that the smoke didn't carry heavy through the flavor. The incredibly rare Scotch had tasting notes of hard candy, icing shortbread, and a dusty brickhouse where it was aged for thirty long, cold years.

Ariel looked at me with a knowing sympathy. "If you need to scream, or if you need a hug, or if you need to cry, I'm here. None of this is easy."

My lips pulled up into a half smile. By the wall lined with giant oak bookshelves, I spotted a small coffee table with two chairs and a well-worn-looking chess set. The simple wood set was so out of place in the incredibly ornate office it was almost comical.

"How about a game?"

"Really? You feel like playing chess right now?"

I spoke quietly, feeling vulnerable, "It's what B-Don and I used to do when we drank together."

She nodded. "Just so you know, I only play for money."

"Well, that's unfortunate because all of my money is at B-Don's house."

Ariel tossed her head back and finished off her glass of whiskey. "The stakes?"

Steeling myself, I drained all of what was left in my glass. The incredibly good whiskey burned its way down my throat. I was not normally so bold, but if you have ever had someone sweep you off your feet, you know exactly how I was feeling. The distraction of how much I wanted Ariel now looked like the only piece of driftwood after a shipwreck. I felt partially guilty for how I felt in this moment, knowing B-Don would never feel anything ever again.

"How about a kiss?"

Ariel smiled a knowing smile. "You're on. But don't think I'm going to take it easy on you just because you're sad right now."

I stood to walk over to the chess set when Ariel exclaimed, "What the fuck are you doing?"

I stuttered mid step and almost fell.

"What's wrong?" I asked.

Ariel shook her empty highball glass with a questioning look on her face. "How the fuck are we going to play chess without a drink in our hands?"

"Well then, bring the bottle."

She pulled the rest of her armor off and was down to a tank top and cargo pants. I couldn't help but notice how beautiful she was. Her muscular form was brutal yet elegant. The fact that this woman was giving me the time of day was mind-boggling to me.

She dug through her desk's bottom drawer. She pulled something out. When she finally came to the small table, bottle and glass in one hand and a chess clock in the other hand, this was the moment when I knew I was in trouble.

I sat down in the chair, resigning myself to my fate. Ariel pulled the cork out of the bottle of whiskey and filled my glass first then filled hers.

She smiled raised her glass and said, "To the kiss you can't possibly win from me."

I smiled, and we clinked glasses.

She set the timer for twenty minutes on each side and said, "Do you want white or black?"

I thought back to my years of playing chess as a child and thought, *White has an advantage.*

I sat back in my chair, trying to conceal my anxiety. "Black."

"Okay." A smile creased her face.

She deftly spun the chessboard so that the black pieces were in front of me.

She sat forward in her chair, whiskey glass in hand. "Start my clock."

I leaned forward and obliged her.

My clock was ticking down, and at the ten-minute mark, I saw something. Her queen was on the same diagonal as her king. I touched my bishop, and a smile swam onto her face that stopped me cold. I decided to stall while I thought.

"Who listens to the death-chip mics?"

Ariel squinted at me in confusion. "Oh… Azrael listens."

I squinted, equally confused. "The who now?"

Ariel laughed. "Azrael is our version of internal affairs. Think of it like HR, but ya know, with guns. They also act as our security force. The chips don't listen. Not actively. There are a preprogrammed set of words or sounds that can cause an alert to sound. We can make them listen if we need to, but…we have twelve thousand employees."

I nodded. The question did its job, and my mind returned fully to the game.

My inner monologue was relentless. *It's a trap. Don't try and pin her queen. She is going to burn your empire to watch the flames dance in your eyes.*

I looked at the pieces laid out in front of me; my head was floating from the whiskey.

I finally decided to just risk it. I moved my bishop.

Ariel said, "Oh no, my queen," with all the eye-rolling sarcasm of a middle-age soccer mom.

Then she moved her rook in for the most obvious checkmate ever given in chess history.

I shook my head, defeated, and began kicking the dog shit out of myself for not seeing that move.

She stood up from her chair and walked over to me. "Good game." She extended her hand.

Like a puppy left out in a rainstorm, I shook it gently.

She grabbed my hand and slowly moved it to her hip. Leaning down, she kissed me gently.

My heart pounded in my ears as her lips touched mine. Shock, surprise, fear, inadequacy all welled up, but stronger than all was curiosity and desire. I pulled her in for more. But she put a knee in my chest, not unkindly.

My head exploded with massive feelings of hope and ecstasy all swirling around a massive grief. She pulled away. At once, I began to form some kind of apology, but a finger quieted my lips before I could speak.

She said in just above a whisper, "Sammi, I like you. I mean I really like you, but we don't know each other yet. It may be in a year that you hate me. Or in a year, I could be dead. Are you ready and prepared to fail like that? Or to suffer like that?"

I shook my head. "No."

She smiled sadly. "Me either."

I was not an impulsive person by nature, but Ariel seemed to drag it out of me. Her very presence felt like jumping off a cliff.

"On second thought." I grabbed her and pulled her to me.

She didn't pull away or hesitate. She leaned down and kissed me again, harder this time. With an almost-apocalyptic desperation, she ripped at my clothes.

"This is a bad idea." She sighed, resigned and lustful.

I laughed as I kissed her neck. "It always is."

"Aw hell," Ariel remarked, pulling her tank top off.

I could feel my heartbeat redlining as the adrenaline screamed through me. I didn't care what happened tomorrow or a month from now. In this moment, my heart was free. And it was full.

In a voice that forbade an inevitable doom, she exhaled, "Fuck it."

— *Chapter 8* —

Aftermath

I SLOWLY WOKE IN an unfamiliar bed, the midday sun blazing through the windows of the fifty-fourth-floor apartment.

As if in a small trickle, like melting ice, the events of the previous day and night flowed back into my mind. I was admiring the view when an arm draped over my chest and a lilting musical voice said, "Good morning."

I was startled. My face turned beet red, and my heart pounded its little adrenaline-fueled song into my ears.

Trying to play off my small panic attack, I said, "Good morning, Ariel."

I turned to face her, and she pulled me into her embrace, kissing me.

"Was yesterday real?" I asked.

She pulled me closer to her and said in a bittersweet timber, "Yes."

"Shit, well, or good, I mean."

She smiled. "Just relax. You aren't scaring me off by being happy or sad. Your friend is dead. I'm not going anywhere. Go for a walk. Mourn and talk to your friends. When B-Don's funeral is over, then we will begin."

"I feel like this is too fast."

She leaned over and grabbed something that got my attention. "If you don't like it, you are free to tell me to stop."

A few minutes passed after we finished for the third time. The gray haze of Seattle started to turn into an opaque orange-yellow glow. The lights of the city fought to escape the mist, but they mixed in on themselves as if embattled.

I realized I had never been hungrier in my life. My stomach rumbled, and Ariel said, "I'm hungry too. Do you want me to have food brought in?"

"Brought in? Like room service?"

She nodded. "We have chefs that prepare all the food for the company round the clock. It may seem excessive, but when you are working eighteen-hour days and sitting through countless meetings, it becomes a necessity."

My phone on the end table rang. Joe's number came up.

"Shit," I said.

Ariel turned to see the phone screen. "Do you know what you are going to say?"

I nodded. "Yeah… I know what I'm going to say."

I slid the green phone icon and put the phone to my ear. "Good morning, you sexy beast."

Joe sounded emotional, which immediately caused me to choke. Tears threatened the corners of my eyes. I forced myself to be silent.

"Sammi, I, uh, hate to be the one to tell you, but something happened. B-Don died last night…in a car crash."

I waited.

"Oh my god… I left him at, like, midnight, and he was in for the night. What happened?"

Joe waited a second, and I could tell he was holding back tears.

"He left to get cigarettes from the gas station by his house, and a pickup truck hit him doing ninety. He died instantly, as did the other driver. The cops called his sister in Florida, who then called me. I'm so sorry, buddy. I know how close you guys were."

"Any idea when the funeral is?"

A long pause followed.

"Not yet. It should be in the next week or so. His sister is coming up here today and will be handling everything. We are having a little get-together here for the employees and friends. That is tomorrow night."

"I'll be there."

There was a long, silent, painful pause.

"Okay, buddy. Call me if you need me."

My voice caught in my throat. "I will. See you tomorrow."

I hung the phone up and sighed. Tears started to leave my eyes silently.

Ariel scrunched up next to me and began comforting me. She rested her head on my shoulder and gently squeezed. The floodgates opened, and I ugly cried. Not that stoic, manly single tear tracing its way down my cheek but sobbing, uncontrollable, gasping, crying. She pulled my head to her chest and squeezed me until all my tears were spent.

She said quietly, "Hey, there is something I need you to do."

— *Chapter 9* —

Othan

AROUND TEN O'CLOCK THE next morning, I left Arrangements by Ariel even though I had no interest in doing so.

I wanted to stay in that bed forever. I was not thinking clearly. The unique combination of infatuation and grief was like taking a sleeping pill and then chasing it with coffee, cocaine, and ecstasy. My mind spun out of control as I trudged to the coffee shop two blocks away from the building.

Ariel had said, "Go to this coffee shop. Ask for Othan, and when he gets there, drink coffee with him. Tell him Vidar sent you. Don't ask him any questions, just listen to what he says."

I had made it to the front of the small, hole-in-the-wall coffee shop, which in Seattle was ubiquitous.

The name on the front door said Valhol Coffee and Imports. Under the name was a symbol that I did not recognize. In white-and-blue knot work, it appeared as three triangles intertwined, with each point slightly lower than the other.

I opened the door, and the room inside was larger than the entrance let on. A large room with varnished, dark, wood floors and soft, almost-nonexistent lighting was filled with the smell of fresh brewed coffee and deserts.

There was a man with a large red beard behind the counter. His stance said, "Get on with it." His brown hair contrasted so greatly with his red beard one of the two groupings of hair must have been dyed.

As I stepped up to the counter, the man said in a pleasant voice, "Good morning, sir. How can we help you today?"

"I was told to come here and ask for Othan. Vidar sent me."

The barista appraised me then, looking at my hands first, then my eyes.

"I will let him know that you are here. If you would please have a seat at the table over by the far wall under the bird symbol."

I looked and saw a small bird drawing on the wall that almost looked like it had been done with chalk.

I went and sat where I was told and waited patiently. After about six minutes had passed, an old man wearing a gray suit, bearing a cane in his right hand, strode from the restroom area.

He was tall, walking smoothly, with the smallest limp in his right leg. His face seemed younger than the rest of his demeanor showed. His gray beard came just to the top of his third button. His eyes seemed to drink in the whole room at once; like a black hole, they pulled everything toward them.

He walked across the room and sat not at my table but the table next to me. He took out his smartphone and ignored me. The old guy must have been in the bathroom when I got here. A long minute passed, and I could feel when I looked away that the old man's right eye seemed to wander over and steal quick glance at me.

He didn't speak to me, so I didn't speak to him when, finally, with the view I had from his right, I saw a small silver chain that was around his neck—the same type of chain that Ariel wore her dagger pendant on.

My mind worked faster than my mouth.

As I started to say something, he turned and said, "Hello, Sami. I...am Othan."

"I was told to come see you by Vidar."

He smiled, and keeping his attention on his smartphone, he said, "I know, but do you always do everything everyone tells you to do?"

"Most of the time, when I can, yes."

"So you are a very agreeable person, you would say?" He made a small gesture to the man behind the coffee counter.

"I suppose that I try to be agreeable when I can be."

Othan nodded and said, "It is as I feared then."

He stood up and sat in the chair across from me. I noticed his left eye was stark white, with a scar running across from the top of his forehead and ending in the middle of his cheek. I couldn't think of a decent response to that, so I waited for him to continue

"Sammi, do you want to know what your problem is?"

I shrugged. "I don't know. But I have a feeling you are about to tell me."

The eyebrow over his right eye raised just enough to make his scar wrinkle a bit. "Sarcasm. Cute. I thought you would be funnier based on your file. Intelligence, it seems, can be measured in different ways."

Not hearing a question or anything to respond to, I remained silent, but the old man was starting to piss me the fuck off.

"Fine, your problem is that no matter what you do next, it will probably lead to a violent and incredibly painful death."

The barista walked over and put two cups of coffee in front of us. Mine looked like it had already been doctored up, so I gave it an exploratory sip. It was perfect in every way. It might have been the best coffee I had ever tasted.

Othan appreciated his coffee and crossed his legs. "How do you feel about that?"

"It scares me. I just watched one of my best, no, one of my only friends die, and dying like that scares me."

The old man nodded and seemed to understand. "Sammi, was that the first time you have ever seen someone die?"

I shook my head.

"Good, then you know the difference between dying with your family around you and dying cold, alone, bleeding out, with no help on the horizon."

My mind flew backward in time, a warehouse, B-Don's eyes begging me for help. Begging me to make it stop. Begging me to tell our captors something that would make it all go away.

"Sammi. Would you like some advice?"

I nodded my head.

"If you listen to me, your life may mean less. But you will have more years of pleasure than of pain. Leave this city tonight. Don't stay for B-Don's funeral. Don't go back to Ariel. Leave it all behind you and go make a quiet life for yourself somewhere."

Othan's eyes appraised me, watching every line on my face for a response.

I recoiled from the idea. I had never wanted anything or anyone the way I wanted Ariel. I had never wanted anything like I wanted to kill Zarov. I stayed in thought, but the old man brought me out of it.

"Do you think that this story that you are on the first page of has a happy ending?"

I shrugged. "I think, there is no such thing as a happy ending. There are only slightly less-sad ones."

The man smiled at this; I could see a thousand lifetimes passing over the old man's face.

"You are correct. We all must die alone. But you can leave something behind. So what will you leave behind you when you are gone, Sammi? A legacy of life or a legacy of death?"

I thought for a moment. "That is a false comparison. It doesn't have to be either-or. The variables are so extreme that I could cure cancer and still be the worst person this planet has ever produced."

The old man took a sip of his coffee and nodded slowly. "I don't think I heard an answer in that very-well-thought-out position statement."

My ears burned. I was sick of this geezer lecturing me like he was my dad. Then realization about his question struck me, and my frustration disappeared.

"You aren't talking about the legacy of life being the quite life. You are talking big picture. You are talking about what the actual literal numbers of lives saved or taken are after I am gone."

The old man smiled a wide smile that showed coffee-stained teeth.

"Very good, Sammi. This life, if you choose it, can lead to an instant and unforgiving death or millions of lives saved. If you understand this, then I wish you luck in whatever you choose, but I give you this warning. No matter what happiness you find, unless you leave now and pretend like none of this ever happened, you will never, for the remainder of your days, find peace that lasts. You will always be haunted by paths not taken and choices made. Until you shut your eyes forever, you will be beset on all sides by enemies. And if you should choose to have them, your children will inherit your demons."

I felt cold chills run up my spine, and the fingers of fear crept into my mind like icy talons. In my fear, there was something else welling up from my stomach. At first, I thought it was anger, but it wasn't. It was resolve. The die was cast. Where it landed was no longer up to me. I had no more of a choice than an apple falling from a tree.

"My choice is made."

He smiled sadly and nodded. "I figured. Go now. I believe there is someone waiting on you back in the tower. Also, try to be less agreeable. That will make you an asshole, but it may keep you alive."

He stood and, with a smooth gait, left the room without another word.

The red-bearded man behind the counter smiled as if he heard every word. I walked out the front door of the coffee shop.

I was now filled with a mountain of anxiety. Fear of the future was not something that I normally struggled with, but now it was pounding in the front of my mind, threatening to give me a headache. In the pain was something true, something not even Othan could take from me—certainty of purpose.

I walked quickly back to the tower, and with the key card Ariel had given me, I nodded to the security guards, scanned my key card, and headed for Ariel's office.

When the elevator opened, I fast walked through the lobby. The receptionist opened the hidden door without even looking up from her computer.

I was angry. I had been dragged into this nonsense by Ariel, and I was done having games played with my head. Did she even like me? Was she using me for some unseen or unknowable purpose? I wanted answers, and I wanted them now.

Sending me to talk with some weird, retired spook that made me feel like my world was crashing down around me even more than it had been earlier in the day was, at best, a dick move. And yet it had given me the certainty I was seeking subconsciously.

I turned the corner, heading down the jade-green hallway, toward the double slabs of oak.

The office right next to her had its door open, and Doc was sitting at his desk.

I asked, "Is she in?"

He stood and walked to me. He gave me a big hug. I was shocked to put it mildly.

"I am so sorry about your friend. If you want to get really drunk and high later to talk, I am here, and I have enough weed and alcohol to kill God."

I hugged him back, some of my anger slipping away. "Thank you. I very well may need that later."

He nodded and said, "She is in. Go on."

I stepped from Doc's office, the Senior Florist title plate passing through my eyeline as I moved. I did not knock on the doors. I pushed them open with all my might. They swung freely on their hinges and moved away from me faster than I intended, but I didn't care.

They boomed against their wall stops, and I said loudly at Ariel, who had jumped up and started toward me, "First of all, how the f——"

She grabbed me and kissed me hard. All my anger drained away, and the anxiety, the fear, all of it left, me in one crystalized moment of bliss. Nothing existed but us for that briefest of moments.

Finally, she pulled away and said, "I am so sorry. I had to be sure."

"I'm not sure. Do that again so I can be sure," I said dreamily.

She punched my arm gently. "I'm sorry. I didn't want to subject you to that, but it needed to be done. If someone can talk to Othan and not get scared off, it means they are solid, and we can depend on them."

I shook my head. "Ya know you have this tracker thing in my arm." I gave my arm a little wave in her direction.

"You could have just, ya know, waited until I split town and click. No more Sammi."

"You are a fucking idiot, but I lo… Thank you for coming back."

I eyed her curiously. "Did you just?"

She punched me again, this time much harder on the arm

"Ow, your lo…hurts."

She smiled. "You have no idea."

I massaged my sore arm. "Do you want to go with me tonight?"

She sat in her giant leather chair. "For security? Probably a good idea. We will trail and follow…"

I shook my head and said, "No, dumbass. I want you to go with me. Like with me, with me."

She shook her head. "That's a massive security problem. Us together in public is not a good idea. I have a social cover as the most eligible bachelorette in Seattle and heiress and all that other bullshit. I am usually noticed when I go places in this city."

I shook my head. "Fine."

I pulled my cell phone out and pulled up the contact that read Break Glass in Case of Hell / Take Ariel to Dinner and pressed the Call icon.

The phone on Ariel's desk rang like an old-school wall phone.

She looked at me incredulously. "Really?"

She picked it up.

"I'm calling in my favor."

She scowled at me. "And what can Arrangements by Ariel do for you, sir?"

"Watch my back when it's dark. Call me on my bullshit when it's needed. Feed me awesome food. Love me till the end of time? Or we can just go out tonight either way."

She smiled broadly. "It's a date."

She hung the phone up and walked over to me and draped her muscular arms around my neck.

"How formal is this get-together?"

"Well, B-Don was a bartender in this town for twenty years. So I am thinking that metal band T-shirts and blue jeans are the order of the day."

"I think I can make that work. All your clothes are in your room, as well as some new clothes. Also, there are some…other things in your room I need to show you."

We walked to the stairwell entrance next to the Norn moot. We descended the two floors to my room and stepped inside. As promised, my clothes were all laying out on the bed, neat and folded.

On the table next to the bed was a long leather case. Ariel walked to the case and unsnapped it.

When she pulled the lid open inside, there were three pistols enclosed in holsters—each larger than the last—and various wicked-looking knives, pill bottles, two watches, and beggaring belief, a tomahawk with a spike on the back and a small protruding claw on the blade.

Ariel deftly picked up the largest of the three pistols and said, "This is a Sig P320 with a red dot. If you are a bit larger, you can conceal this, as it is the most forgiving of the three. Those two are the SIG P365 XL and P365, smaller, but they hold less ammo, and their recoil is harder to control. Blades are not primary weapons unless silence is needed, but this is just for tonight, so I doubt that will be the case. Pistols are only so you can fight to a rifle. These are all yours until your training starts. Then you will have a better idea of what you want. Until then, pick one pistol and one blade."

I looked at the arrangement in front of me. I was completely out of my depth. I picked up the tomahawk, surprised at how light it was, and gave my best Ragnar impression.

"Power is always there for those that can humble themselves and pick it up."

She snorted. "I'm pretty sure you butchered that."

Smiling, I agreed, "I am pretty sure I did too."

I picked up a black, rectangle-looking thing, with an eagle's claw on the side of it.

I slid up the mechanism on the side, and a 4.5-inch blade shot out the end of it, and I smiled.

"Okay, this thing is fucking awesome."

She smiled. "Good choice. Microtech Halo VI—fast, but not silent. Something to keep in mind."

I tried to close it but couldn't figure out how.

Ariel said, "Let me."

I handed it to her, and she pulled the butt of the knife down, and the blade disappeared.

I nodded and slid the knife into my pocket.

I picked up the largest of the three pistols, and she said, "Any idea how to put that on?"

I shook my head.

"Okay, basically, you have two good choices on how to carry it. You can carry it appendix, so just to the right of your belt buckle. It's faster, but you have to carry a gun pointed at your dick. The most popular way is to carry at the four o'clock just past your hip. It's slower, but you don't have a gun pointed at your dick."

"I am relatively attached to my dick, and I think it's possible you might be his second biggest fan."

She blushed. "You are correct."

She stepped around me and pulled my shirt up, quickly tucking the pistol into my right hip and snapping the clips over my belt.

She nodded. "Okay, try and draw it."

I pulled my shirt up and clumsily pulled the gun out. I felt slow.

"Not bad," she said. "Try pulling up your shirt up to your chest and, with your other hand, grab the gun."

I put the gun back in the holster and tried it her way. It was faster.

She nodded. "Better. Not great, but better."

She stepped behind me, pulling the gun from the holster. Walking back to the case, she pulled out three magazines and deftly loaded the magazine into the firearm and racked the slide back. She pulled the slide back a little, checked the breach, and then put the gun back in the holster.

"Whoa! That's loaded. Shouldn't I keep it unloaded until I need it?"

She looked at me, confused, then realization dawned on her.

"You mean there is one in the chamber?"

She nodded in understanding. "No, you always carry with one in the chamber. Having to rack the slide in a fight is death. You draw attention to yourself when you rack the slide like you are in an eighties action movie. One in the pipe always unless you are a fan of carrying a very complicated paperweight around on your hip."

"But couldn't it go off accidently?"

"Ugh." Ariel rubbed her eyes as if my statement gave her a migraine. "Sorry. It's not you. This is one of the silliest things that non-gun people think." She made little air quotes. "I can rack the slide fast enough. You can't. No one can. If the person you are fighting is trained, it is most fucking certainly a death sentence."

"Okay."

"You probably won't need it tonight, but If I am going with you, I want you armed, but you don't take either of them out until I'm no longer in a position to help you, or I tell you too. Got it?"

I nodded.

"I'm getting a shower and then getting dressed."

"Okay," I said.

She looked at me like I was an absolute idiot.

"This is the part where you ask me if I want some company."

I almost choked on my tongue as the excitement and adventure that was Ariel filled my soul like aloe on a burn. "Oh, you mean… Oh, got it."

She laughed and said, "I swear I took advantage of you. Just a babe in the woods, lost and alone, and I came along and corrupted your pure, monk-like essence."

"That is pretty much what happened."

She walked in the bathroom and made a show of sticking her arm around the corner and letting her T-shirt drop off one extended finger.

I immediately started unlacing my boots.

— Chapter 10 —

A Party Worth Forgetting

Ariel departed after our shower to some unknown corner of the building, where she was presumably getting ready.

After a few minutes, I selected my Sabaton T-shirt and my trusty pair of Lucky jeans, which I realized I had been wearing for three days straight.

I finished by putting on the gun the way Ariel had shown me. The knife I selected felt good in my pocket. A paranoia began to build at the back of my mind.

You have a loaded firearm in your pants. You are going to shoot your ass off. Throw the gun in the trash lest you rearrange your (or someone else's) insides.

"Shut the fuck up," I said out loud to myself.

I turned on music on my phone and gave the handgun a reassuring pat to make sure it was still there.

My phone's music cut out, and it buzzed its little vibrating hymn. I picked up.

"You almost ready? I hate to be that girl. But I did steal your soul a few minutes ago. Just making sure you are still on task." I could hear the smile in her voice.

"I'll be down in three minutes. Should I go to—"

Ariel cut in, "The motor pools. Not the parking garage."

"See you in two."

I stood up, gathered what little I had, and headed for the elevator down to the subterranean motor pool.

Ariel was waiting for me by the elevator, wearing a Black Label Society T-shirt.

Arrangements by Ariel

She walked over and grabbed my hand. "Tell me you are a history nerd without telling me you are a history nerd."

I smiled. "Tell me you are secret biker girl without telling me you are a secret biker girl."

As we walked down the row of black Suburbans, other smaller and larger vehicles began to flank our left and right.

She pointed to a vehicle at the end of the row and spoke, "That's our ride."

I did not recognize the vehicle. Ariel noticed this.

"2022 Rolls-Royce Ghost. This one has been customized to fit our company a little better than the standard model."

I looked at her incredulously. "Do try to bring it back in one piece this time, 007."

She snorted a laugh. She pressed a button on the car remote. The engine started, and all four doors opened. I sat in the passenger seat, and my door automatically closed.

Ariel sat down in the seat next to me, and her door swung closed. As Ariel grabbed her seat belt, a soothing electronic female voice spoke from what felt like all around us.

"Good evening, Ariel and unknown passenger. The weather this evening is sixty-five degrees, with mild precipitation. Visibility is limited at four hundred meters. Ladar and radar are fully functional. Connection to TOC established. Electronic countermeasures online. Trophy system online. Ammunition counts full. Is there anything else needed this evening?"

Ariel smiled and said, "Good evening, KITT. If you would please introduce yourself to Sammi, my boyfriend."

I mouthed, "Boyfriend?"

Ariel smiled and shook her head at me.

The voice responded quickly, "Hello, Sammi. I am KITT. I am a—"

"Hello, KITT. I know what you are. I have seen *Nightrider*."

The voice responded freakishly fast, "Hahaha, well, with respect to my predecessor, old KITT ain't got shit on me."

I looked at Ariel with a mix of awe, fear, and holy shit. Ariel smiled at me.

"KITT is a tactical AI. She supplies real-time information in dynamic and nondynamic situations. She does everything."

"How is the sound system in this thing?"

Horror crossed Ariel's face.

"Oh no..."

But her words were drowned out by the sound of "Killing in the Name" by Rage Against the Machine, which conveniently came in on the "Fuck you, I won't do what you tell me" part. The bass boomed. And the windows shook. Ariel reached over and pressed the Off button on the large touch screen.

"Fuck you, KITT," she yelled and rubbed her ears.

"Oh, I'm sorry. Did I hurt the meat bag's wittle ears?"

I looked at Ariel with, "What the fuck?" written all over my face.

Ariel said, "HK47 programing off. Standard operation only."

KITT said, "Confirmed. Standard operating procedure activated. What are the mission parameters?"

"Protection of both passengers highest priority. Zero electronic footprint."

"Confirmed. Please state your destination."

"Sarajevo Night Club."

KITT's interior lights darkened, and the large screen lit up on the dash. Ariel removed her hands from the wheel, and the car pulled out of the parking space.

"Well, this thing is bananas."

Ariel nodded and said, "Wait until you see the mini gun."

I looked at her skeptically. "Really?"

"Really, really."

Ariel pulled her gun from its holster that she wore appendix. She press-checked the handgun and, seeing a round in the chamber, put it back in her holster.

I looked at her, thinking of how routine this must be for her.

"Have I told you how hot it is watching you play with guns?"

"You have failed to mention that up to this point."

"Well, it is. Also, it makes sense you carry there. No dick to shoot off."

She laughed, stifling a snort. "You almost sound disappointed."

I blushed and raised my hands in surrender. "Nope. No disappointment over here."

She giggled.

The car wound its way up the ramp and out into the gray Seattle air.

Ariel said, "KITT, activate EHUD."

A small electronic whir sounded as the windows and windshield were covered with lines that outlined everything, emphasizing structures. The windows were creating an augmented reality. It was surreal. The cityscape became instantly translated into enhanced images that were clear and easy to understand.

Ariel said, "It also works on people."

I looked closer, and all the people on the sidewalk were also outlined in green. One turned yellow for a second.

"Why did that one turn yellow?"

Ariel nodded in that person's direction. "The system analyzes body position and determines threat level based on hand-movement speed of movement and estimated vision alignment. When someone does something the computer doesn't like, they turn yellow. And if they do something it really doesn't like, they turn red."

"What happens when they turn red?"

She smiled. "Well…that depends on what they do immediately after they turn red."

This augmented reality was jarring at first, but somehow intuitive and easier to understand the longer you looked.

The car made the last turn. Ariel assumed control of the vehicle as they pulled into the parking lot, as she obviously didn't trust KITT to park them without running over any "meat bags."

"Afraid Skynet here is going to take someone out?"

"HK47 mode disabled response redacted."

"I think that is her currently shackled way of telling you to go fuck yourself."

"Thanks, I caught that."

Ariel pulled into one of the last spots available.

"Looks like this is going to not be such a low-key affair after all."

Ariel nodded. "Looks that way. Okay, let's go over our E and E plan."

I stared blankly. "Our what now?"

Ariel sighed. "Escape and evasion plan. If something goes sideways, whoever gets to the car first will say, 'KITT, find partner.' The car will then navigate to the other person, and we will get the hell out. Good?"

I nodded.

Ariel cracked her knuckles. "Okay, let's do this."

We stepped from the vehicle, and Ariel took my right hand in her left, her eyes searching left and right as we walked.

"Hey, what happened to all of that money you gave me that was at B-Don's house?"

She smiled. "B-Don's will left it to a charity that helps underprivileged kids get into music."

My eyes raised. "No shit?"

"Yeah, we put a will together for him that would take care of everything seamlessly."

A smile, a sad one, swam onto my face. "He would have liked that."

We stepped into the nightclub. A sign on the front door read, "Closed for a private party."

The party seemed anything but private. Every bouncer, bartender, barback, and bottle girl and boy from Seattle seemed to be in attendance.

There was a woman on the stage with an acoustic guitar that was playing some soothing alternative music and singing confidently but quietly into the mic. We walked to the bar, and some friends of ours from another club were bartending while all the bartenders from the nightclub were obviously already drunk.

Someone walked over to us. I didn't recognize her.

"Oh my god. You are Ariel Vidar, aren't you?"

Ariel waved her hand and said, "Oh, hi, um, no, I don't think I know who that is."

The women looked confused as we walked past and over to the corner of the bar.

"Why are you famous exactly?"

She shook her head, sighing at the thought. "I am famous because of my father's fortune and my scientific work."

I looked at her quizzically. She sighed again and said, "I'm a botanist by trade. My claim to fame is, I made a hybrid of the Kadupul flower that lasts for an entire season instead of just wilting and dying overnight. Which made the company millions. Forbes published an article a couple of years ago called 'Queen of the Night,' another name for the flower. Which put me in the public eye. At that point, though, I was operations only, no fieldwork. Obviously, it has had some unintended consequences."

Joe walked over from sitting in the VIP section and gave me a big hug. "Hey, buddy, who's your friend?"

"Joe this is…"

Ariel stuck her hand out and said, "Ariel, girlfriend."

Joe looked at us in disbelief. He laughed and said "You are dating this guy? Why the…"

Ariel made eye contact with Joe. She held her hands about a foot apart and gave him a nod. "For his money, of course."

Joe ugly laughed and said, "Oh, buddy, she is so fucking out of your league."

"I can't argue with you. Out of my league doesn't really begin to do it justice. I think out of my dimension would be more accurate."

Joe nodded and said, "Ha! You crazy kids have fun. I gotta go do a speech in a minute. Can you go make sure Alex is still alive?"

I smiled. "No problem. Is he in VIP?"

Joe nodded and moved toward the stage. The bartender walked over, and we both ordered a light beer. We walked toward the VIP section and saw Alex holding on to the handrail and Weeble wobbling.

"How you doing, buddy?"

He squinted at me. "Just trying not to fall over. How 'bout you?"

"About the same."

The music stopped, and Joe took the stage. Mic in hand, he was the epitome of a showman. But you could tell this was hard.

"Friends, loved ones, and everyone else who shouldn't be here."

This got a laugh from the irreverent crowd.

"We are here to remember and drink copiously in tribute to Brendon Wheeler. One of the kindest, most loyal, and meaningful friends anyone could have had. Now, in true B-Don fashion, I don't want to see a hand without a drink in it tonight. This night is for all of us to do what B-Don loved most. To drink a little drink, smoke a little smoke, and listen to all of the local musicians that he loved so much play their tunes. But over everything, have fun. Let your freak flags fly. Drink as much as you want. The cops have been bribed."

The crowd was devolving into bittersweet laughter.

"The city commissioner has been threatened, and all of us tonight in this building will drink more than one toast to the very sweetest of our friends. Here's to B-Don."

The crowd raised their drinks and answered in a roar, "To B-Don."

Silence fell as drinks were downed across the club. Joe handed the mic back to the lady with the acoustic guitar. Music began to drift through the club again. This time, it was a little harder, less softness around the edges of it.

Ariel leaned over to me. "Look at the mic stand at the corner of the stage."

I looked, and there on top of the mic stand was one of B-Don's most signature items, a fedora.

Tears welled in my eyes, and I sat down and let the tears flow. I sipped my beer, and Ariel sat down next to me, holding my hand, comforting me. We sat like that, watching the musician play her heart out.

I felt Ariel's hand tighten around mine, jolting me out of my revere.

"Front door. Two guys, one in a grey hoodie, the other with a red-and-black T-shirt."

I saw them. They couldn't have stood out more if they tried from the eclectic crowd.

"I think it's time for us to leave."

I nodded, looking at Alex. "Alex, you okay, buddy?" but Alex had passed out in the chair to Ariel's right.

I heard the words of Othan in my head. "Leave this city right now and make a quiet life for yourself somewhere."

I banished the words from my mind. I was committed.

Ariel stood and pulled her smartphone out. As we walked down the stairs toward the back exit. A man wearing a blue raincoat stood between us and the exit. He locked eyes with me and then looked at Ariel. His eyes betrayed recognition, and Ariel was in motion before the man had made up his mind on what to do next.

Ariel plowed into the man in a picture-perfect double-leg takedown.

My heart leapt into my throat, and it pounded blood into my ears. I registered that the woman that I was in rapturous love with was now fighting a man that outweighed her by fifty pounds.

I struggled for a second for my gun, but then I saw her hand go to the small of her back and return, sliding a knife into the center of the man's throat. He gasped and wheezed as the blade found its home in his esophagus.

Ariel turned, postured up, and dragged the man out the back entrance of the club.

The man was still fighting for control of the knife, which clattered to the pavement in the alley.

I didn't know what to do to help, so I looked around for more bad guys. Seeing none, I turned to see if I could help Ariel. The man was now rising to his feet, clawing and pulling at Ariel's hair. Ariel raised her hand to her ear, putting her elbow in the man's already-wounded neck. With one swift motion, she pulled her pistol from the holster. She wrapped a thumb around the back of the small pistol. She placed the muzzle directly on the man's chest and fired.

He fell backward, grabbing soundlessly at his chest. Ariel tapped the magazine and racked the slide backward aggressively, ejecting the spent cartridge. She leveled the gun at the man, but he was obviously out of the fight. She looked around for other threats. Seeing none, she changed the magazine on her pistol and returned it to its holster.

My adrenaline was through the roof. I couldn't form words or do anything other than breathe rapidly.

"Are you good?"

This snapped me out of my frozen state. "Yeah."

She nodded she walked over to a dumpster. She grabbed a large, broken-down box. She placed it over the man's broken and motionless body.

A few seconds later, the car pulled up in front of us. The two front doors opened. We jumped inside.

"Holy shit," I remarked.

Ariel reached into the back seat and pulled out a rifle. She pulled the bolt back slightly, confirming a round was in the chamber.

"We aren't out of this yet. KITT, scan area for anomalous behavior."

A *chink, chink* sound came from the trunk; small drones shot out of hidden doors. Real-time imaging came up on the screen, and KITT's voice filled the car, "Estimated ten combatants in three vehicles converging on our location."

All the vehicles in question lit up like little red dots on a videogame mini map. KITT was right. All the vehicles split off, but they were coming right for us.

Ariel said calmly, "Okay, KITT. Let's find somewhere out of the way where a few gunshots won't bother anyone."

KITT's voice responded quickly, "Three locations updated to Map."

Ariel scrolled through the locations quickly.

"TOC, this is Dagger Actual. Do you read?"

A male voice came from the ceiling of the vehicle. "Reading you, Lemma Charlie Dagger Actual. We confirm three victors are in route to interdict. Three counter-ambush locations. Best choice is a fishing port five point three miles from your location No overnight traffic for another eight hours estimated. Recommend you proceed there at best speed."

Ariel responded, "Copy. All Dagger elements converge on location. Prepare clean and wrap protocol."

A chorus of voices responded quickly but orderly.

"Dagger 6 copies."

"Dagger 5 copies."

My head was spinning as my heart redlined.

"Is there anything I should do?"

Ariel said, "Yes, when we get there, I am going to need you to stay very quiet and very calm. This was part of Zarov's plan, I think. Capitalize on your dead friend, lure you back out into the open, and then take you out and whoever was with you. He might not get the answers he wants but he can show his clients a body to make them confident that his house is in order once again. Honestly, I expected him to hit the funeral, not this get-together."

I was shaking like a leaf, with no control over my quaking hands.

"So what do we do now?"

"We are going to let these guys follow us, and then we are going to kill them, hopefully save one for interrogation."

I nodded and let out a breath I didn't realize that I was holding.

She reached over and grabbed my hand. "Don't worry, babe. They picked the wrong girl's date to ruin." She gave me a little wink.

This made me giggle just a little, and the spell of the situation was partially broken. I pulled my gun from behind my back.

"Ready."

She laughed. "Babe, put that away. With what we are about to do to them, you won't need that."

We plowed through a locked gate that snapped open as we knocked it aside. The augmented reality of the car's windshield and windows painted the surrounding landscape with little green lines, showing the blocky outlines of cargo containers as we pulled through the entrance.

On top of the containers, little blue triangles floated. Ariel took control of the vehicle and pulled into position at the end of the pier and in perfect eyeline to the front gate.

A few moments later, the vehicles that were outlined in red pulled through the gate and split into a V formation, spaced thirty feet apart. They in unison stopped and pulled to the right, hiding the figures exit from the vehicle. In three seconds, they exited behind shields and began moving toward our vehicle.

My heart leapt back into my throat as they closed to one hundred yards. Ariel raised her hands in surrender.

Ariel whispered, "Raise your hands."

I did so.

"KITT, activate HK47 protocol. Kill all meat bags save one."

A clinking and whirring sound went through the car. The interior lights changed from a cool blue to red, and Ariel said, "Cover your ears. All Dagger elements execute."

In simultaneous astonishment from myself and our attackers, a screaming *brrrt* sounded from the mini gun that just appeared out of the hood of our vehicle as if from nowhere. Tracer rounds hurtled their deadly light into the men and chewed them up like a lawn mower.

Rockets streaked from the top of the containers, and the SUVs behind them exploded, and surprisingly, there was very little fire.

The attackers fell and tried to scatter from the withering barrage, but they all fell like marionette dolls that had just had their strings cut.

Just as quickly as it started, it was over. The mini gun smoked, but barked no more. The smoke drifted from the barrels and danced away on the slow breeze. It just as quickly sank back into its housing, a little hatch closing over the top of it. One man was crawling back toward the vehicles. Six figures appeared from behind the containers, rifles in hand—one carrying a large, belt-fed machine gun—all wearing the helmets that I recognized from the other night.

They moved, increasing the space between them, scanning for more targets. They converged on a squirming, screaming man and zip-tied his hands behind his back.

The guy in the rear of the figures all outlined in blue from the augmented reality windshields ran and took a knee next to the wounded man. He cut off the man's shirt and pants deftly with trauma shears and began stuffing a hole in the man's shoulder with gauze. He then inspected the wounds, nodded to one of the other men, and he made a little circle motion with his finger.

Ariel opened her car door and stepped out. She slung her rifle over her shoulder with practiced ease. I jumped out of the car and followed her.

"Doc, how is he?"

An electronic voice answered, "Stable. Needs medical in the next hour."

"Alright, commence SSE and get Azrael over here to clean this shit up."

They all nodded.

"Meet back at the tower for debrief one hour."

They all nodded again.

She pulled out her cell phone and placed it to her ear. "Skuld, full moot, two hours." She ended the call. "You sure know how to show a girl a good time."

I was trying not to barf from the smell of the dead men on the ground. Their shields had been bent and dented by the spray of bullets from the car. Their bodies were laying at unnatural angles.

I stifled a dry heave. Trying to disguise my revulsion and disgust for the scene laid out before me, I said, "Remind me never to piss that car off."

"Yeah, that would be a bad idea."

We sat back down in our car.

"Honeymoon is over, babe. Your training starts tomorrow."

I nodded and checked the time. 10:50 p.m. Less than thirty minutes had passed since we left the nightclub. It felt like a lifetime ago.

"I have a lot of questions about what just happened."

She nodded, but addressed the car first. "KITT, take us home."

The car beeped, and the lights in the interior that were red went back to blue. The car responded, "All meat bags have been dealt with. I think I deserve a new air freshener."

Ariel rolled her eyes. "I'll get right on that."

"I saw that," KITT said.

The car started toward the exit gate, and I asked, "Why did you put your thumb over the back of your pistol when you shot that guy in the alley?"

Ariel laughed bitterly. "That is your first question? Not how did the guys get on top of the containers? How did they track us when they were too far behind us? Nothing about the fact that we have a car with an auto-targeting mini gun?"

I shrugged and said, "I don't know. It just was kind of a standout from all the other stuff."

She shook her head in astonishment, giggled, and said, "When you shoot someone at point-blank range like that, a lot of stuff blows backward and gets caught in the slide, and it can make your firearm useless, so best thing to do is make sure the action doesn't move and then rerack after the shot is fired."

"Do you often put your gun up against people when you shoot them?"

"No, that was a first for me, but our training is very comprehensive, and we drill it so often that it is just part of our DNA."

"Are you okay?" Noticing the blood on her face and arms, worry creased my face.

She paused and thought for a moment. "Yeah, I think so. I will get checked a little later to be sure."

The car sped toward the tower, and a headache started to pound in my head, and I felt so sleepy. I started nodding off mid-conversation.

"You are coming down from the adrenaline." She reached behind my seat. "Drink this. Hold a little of it in your mouth for a few minutes to speed up the effect."

Taking what looked like a bottle of water in my hand, I asked, "What's in it?"

"Electrolyte water and a strong stimulant. We call it combat water. Only drink a couple of mouthfuls."

I nodded and drank. Within a few minutes, I was feeling better. The headache started to fade.

"Will it be like this forever?"

She looked at the celling of the car, considering. "No, not forever. Your training starts tomorrow. Focus on that, and the rest will work itself out."

Othan's words echoed in my head. *You will never know peace that lasts.*

I sat quietly for a minute, and Ariel said, "We have some work to do when we get back, but when that's done, we should play some chess."

I nodded, and my mood brightened at the change to a positive topic. I couldn't tell if it was because I was glad or if the night's events were just so fucked anything normal sounded pleasant.

The rest of the drive was silent. We pulled into the motor pool, and Ariel deftly parked the car in its parking spot.

"Have a pleasant night, meat bags," KITT said.

"Disable HK47 protocol."

I smiled. "I didn't say earlier because my mind was too busy, but that reference is hilarious."

Ariel smiled broadly. "I thought you might get it. Did you play light side or dark side in KOTOR?"

I giggled. "Both. But played more dark than light."

She nodded. "Makes sense."

I asked, "How about you?"

"I have literally played that game into the dirt with a hundred playthroughs half-light half dark side," she said.

My eyes widened. "Holy shit. Did it at least give you a degree with that level of commitment?"

She shook her head. "Sadly, all it did was make me hypercritical of every Star Wars game that came after it. Come on, let's get a beer and head up."

I followed her toward the elevators, and before we got there, she took a right, and we walked over to a fridge that's only purpose seemed to be to hold beer.

Hanging on the front of a fridge was a dry-erase board with a litany of names on it, with Xs next to each name. At the top of the white board was written, "Postmortem Beers." Doc's name had the most Xs by far next to it, but Ariel's had the second most. She put two Xs next to her name and opened the fridge and retrieved two light beers.

Hanging from a line of paracord on the side of the fridge, with its breach open, was a small handgun; on the slide, it read, "Makarov." She slid the frame of the pistol under the bottle cap and snapped it upward, popping the cap of, and repeated the action on the second bottle.

She handed me the bottle, and I took it.

She clinked her bottle against mine, saying, "Nihil vivit aut frustra moritur. Nothing lives or dies in vain."

We drank deeply and then walked to the elevator.

— *Chapter 11* —

Norn Moot

ARIEL AND I HEADED from the elevator to a conference room in the middle of the office building labeled Briefing Room.

Ariel stopped at her office to retrieve a laptop. We walked in, beers in hand, and sat. About fifteen minutes later, all six of the operators from the ambush walked in, helmets and beers in hand. They sat around the table.

Ariel said, "Let's make this quick. We have the moot assembled, and I have to be in there in thirty minutes. Doc, how is our prisoner?"

Doc took a swig of his beer. "Talkative actually. We just got his file back from Azrael, and his name is Derek Lasky. The guy is a mercenary out of Montenegro. He has some ties to the Russian mob, but mostly works for companies in the liquidation and asset-acquisition field. He so far has given up that he is from South Africa and didn't know who the targets were, just a couple pictures, a time, and address. They had drone support, which explains why they were able to track you so well. Mr. Lasky has been moved to interrogation, and we expect some results by tomorrow morning "

Ariel nodded. "Makes sense, Doc. Before you go home, call our office in Montenegro and get Dmitri running down the broker. I want to know who hired this guy. Phill, was infill and ex-fill smooth?"

Phill nodded. "QRF chopper dropped us off on the containers and picked us up after the barge scrapped the SUVs. Time on target was 13:12. We have done better but have also done worse."

Another guy across the table said, "You've done worse."

This got a small laugh from everyone.

"Bobby, what about sig int. Did we get anything off the drone's transmission?"

A large man sitting across from Doc shook his head. "No, they were simple but efficient versions. Closed circuit, so they were not recording best we can tell. So we should be clean on that front. As far as counter measures went, KITT's electronic warfare suite did its job. Nothing should be left to tie you guys to the scene."

Ariel nodded. "Petra, talk to me about SSE."

A small-framed woman with auburn hair leaned forward. "Kryptal phones with AES–128 encryption. IT has them and is trying to crack them now. Obviously, that is going to take some time if it's possible at all. Based on the other profiles of the assault team, it looks like this was set up as non-attributable. Nothing on the vehicles, but some of these knuckle draggers helped cook anything that might have been in there."

This generated laughs from all the skull crushers sitting around the table.

Ariel smiled. "Sammi, this is Direct-Action Team Dagger. The two over there are Rook and Eli."

Both men gave me a little nod, and I nodded back.

Ariel wrapped up the meeting. "Everyone, stay in contact with Azrael to tighten up any loose ends, and enjoy the rest of your evening. You are all welcome at the moot, but I know how much you enjoy those things. So feel free to fuck off at your leisure. Beautiful job tonight."

Ariel stood. Everyone around the table stood in unison.

"Feather or Heart," Ariel said sternly.

They responded loudly and in unison, "We balance the scales!"

The hair on my arm stood up at attention as if it was responding to the actions of everyone else in the room.

Team Dagger all filed out of the conference room and headed in different directions, talking and laughing like this was just a day at the office. I realized that, for them, that is exactly what it was. I felt like I had been shoved into a weird sitcom that had nothing but psychopaths for characters.

Ariel took a right and headed toward the sealed entrance of the Norn moot. The scales of Anubis blazed bright on the entrance. As Ariel stepped closer, the wall split on its seam. Sound, motion, and light poured through the opening.

Sixty people, all wearing various qualities of clothing, milled around the room and sat in what looked like assigned seats.

Two older women and one older man all walked onto the stage and sat in their large leather chairs.

Ariel motioned to some seats along the back wall. "Sit in one of those seats. I have to address the moot first, and then I'll come sit with you."

I moved to sit.

Ariel walked down the center aisle and took the stage. She walked to the dais and set her laptop on the large lectern with a wood carving of the scales of Anubis on it.

Ariel began, "Good evening, everyone. Thank you all so much for being here. Tonight there was an attack on my person and that of our newest recruit. This attack was a direct second order effect of the unfortunate death of Edward Gallo."

This managed to illicit some laughter in the room, which was so unexpected I almost busted out laughing too.

Ariel continued, "The only item on the table tonight is the immediate termination of Gallo's number-two man who has taken over his business."

She pulled up a security camera image of the man in the blue suit. My blood boiled, and my hands clinched into fists. Just seeing him sent my heart into overdrive.

Ariel continued, "This is Marquis Zarov. I believe you were supplied a briefing on him by Skuld remotely yesterday."

Heads across the room nodded.

"Good. I'll turn it over to Skuld, and he will begin with the initial vote. Then he will field arguments for and against if any are on offer. Again, thank you all for coming. Your service is what keeps this organization pure and accountable."

She closed the file folder and stepped from the dais.

A man that looked to be in his late eighties stepped up.

"Good evening to my fellow Norns and members of the moot. If you will indulge an old man, something all of you probably know. The game we play is Bayesian in nature. By its very definition, the outcome as always has more than two players influencing it. Consider that we thought Gallo's relatively small organization would resort to infighting and, in so doing, lose most of its power. Obviously, that prediction was incorrect. So now we are regathered to walk in our aim. Is this Zarov a chimera eating his own tail, or is he a seed that will sprout into something just as bad or worse than Edward Gallo?"

Ariel sat down next to me and slid her hand into mine.

"What the fuck is Bayesian?"

She smiled and shook her head. "Google it."

Skuld continued, "With all the possible variables included and possible third and fourth order effects in mind, please cast your preliminary votes."

The screen changed to a large representation of the scales of Anubis, with a feather on one side and a heart on the other side.

On each side of the scale was sixty small white boxes, with numbers one to sixty on each box. The room was silent as all the members of the moot scrolled through their tablets, some shaking their heads in thought; others played with long beards or adjusted their glasses.

A timer set for five minutes appeared on the screen. Skuld left the podium and took his seat in the middle of the three Norns. Some kind of tribal music started playing from the ceiling.

Ariel leaned over. "The voting is based on how many change their minds. If everyone votes yes in the preliminary debate, then if 20 percent vote no, the nos take it, and vice versa. The threshold is 15 percent. If the threshold is exact, then the Norns vote and break the tie."

I nodded my understanding. "How do you think this is going to go?"

She smiled a crooked smile. "Quickly."

The clock counted down the last few seconds, then all the votes were in.

The count was forty-five for the motion to kill Zarov and fifteen against.

Skuld walked back to the stage. "To oppose the motion for assassination as always is Urd. Ten minutes on the clock, please."

The elderly woman in the chair farthest to the left moved to the podium. The clock started as soon as she started talking.

"Good evening to all. This man is not worthy of death for two reasons. The first you have all heard me state hundreds of times. We are not capable, even with all our organization's illustrious trappings, of deciding who lives and who dies. This man is a small fish in a very big pond. He is not worth our time or our attention. Gallo was the brain. This man is at very best a minor annoyance. His actions thus far have been clumsy, even bungling. Not one of our direct-action teams have taken a casualty at his hands, and his body count thus far since this caper began is one. As our counterparts in accounting know, staging something like this kidnapping and interrogation, and the assault on Ariel and Sammi tonight, is not cheap. I doubt he has the resources to try again."

I almost flew out of my seat in anger. Ariel's calm hand on my forearm stopped me.

"Point of order."

Ariel stood.

Skuld stood briefly. His voice boomed in the chamber. "The chair recognizes Ariel Vidar."

Ariel spoke tersely, "Marquis Zarov has been fighting wars or starting them for twenty years. He worked as Gallo's number two for ten of those years. Gallo's net worth was over seven hundred million dollars. There is no reason to believe that he has not drained those accounts into his own. In fact, we have reason to suspect Gallo being in Seattle, in the open, was Zarov's doing. He was here for personal reasons, but there is no reason to think that Zarov himself could not or would not have made the intel for us. Unavoidable."

Ariel sat down. The older lady looked to Skuld. Skuld nodded for her to continue.

"Ariel may have a point. But this does not mean that this action has been measured appropriately. If we kill Zarov, what is the endgame? We tracked and killed Nazis for years after the war."

Skuld smiled and stated loud enough for anyone to hear. "Good times."

This got a laugh from the room.

Urd continued, "To my second reason, this path has no end. We cannot keep the scales balanced if every time some upstart lowlife pops up gets put down by us like playing a game of Whac-A-Mole. Every time that we act, we risk exposing ourselves to the public and all the nations of the world. Even we, the ones that have loved the stars too fondly to be fearful of the night, cannot long escape the public gaze of the world powers. For these and so many other reasons, I ask you who voted yes to change your vote to no and give Zarov the greatest indignity any enemy can suffer. To be ignored. I yield the rest of my time."

The woman's words made a certain kind of sense to me even though I was angrier than hell at her for daring to minimize my friend's death so profoundly.

Skuld walked to the dais and up to the podium. "I now call to the podium Verdandi to speak in the affirmative."

The thin women in the seat on the right stood. The screen behind her started scrolling quickly through images. All of them were horrible.

A man with no arms being dragged through the street.

Another man with a tire around his arms and waist on fire.

Bodies piled in graves.

The images continued for several minutes. Finally, she spoke. I was surprised at how deep her voice was.

"Good evening. Those pictures you just saw were indeed ordered by Edward Gallo, but who was his man in the field? Who struck the zippo that burned that man in front of his family? Who gave the order to massacre the village in Mali? Who attacked the funeral? My eternal interlocutor said there was only one body with Zarov's name on it. You can order someone to do something until you turn blue. The person who pulls the trigger is as, if not more, responsible than the one who makes the plan and orders them forward. His actual body count is north of eighteen hundred. With this information in mind, turn your attention, if you would, on tonight. The only reason

Sammi and Ariel aren't dead is because the men he hired botched the job. Instead of patiently waiting for them to walk to their car, they tried to flush them out. So is he a clear and present danger to innocent people? Well, considering that he has killed someone innocent personally in the last two days, I think that question answers itself. Vote yes, let's cut his throat, and be done with it." Verdandi sat back down next to Skuld.

Ariel smiled at me, watching my reaction. "Having fun yet?"

"Actually, yeah. I feel like they would be taking longer if it wasn't the middle of the night."

She giggled quietly. "Yeah, most of them are not as spry as they used to be."

Skuld returned to the podium. "Are there any arguments that would be voiced?" He paused, eyeing everyone in the crowd. "So noted. Three minutes for the final vote. Feather or heart."

The crowd responded, "We balance the scales."

Skuld sat.

Ariel rubbed my arm and said, "You know it will take us a while to find him. Don't think about it. Put yourself wholly into your training, and let all this other shit sit by the wayside for a while."

I caressed her hand in little figure-eight patterns.

"Got it. Do I get one of those neat helmets you guys have?"

Her smile was beaming. "You are getting yours tomorrow. They are called Ronin V5s. We bought the patent about eight years back, and they never made it to the general market. The guys that made it work for us now and basically spend all day making new ones and shipping them to our offices all over the world. The version 2 is still in production so that, if ever caught on video, they don't raise too much suspicion."

"That makes sense," I said.

The timer reached ten seconds and then disappeared. I assumed correctly that meant all votes were in.

Skuld moved to the podium. The graphic of the scales moved, and the heart sank, with the feather raising toward the top left of the screen.

He said without ceremony, "The change comes to 10 percent. The Aye's have it. Verdandi, draft the order, sign it, seal it, and deliver it to the Vidar."

Verdandi reached under the table and pulled out something I had never seen before. It was a small bowl suspended over a candle that was already lit. Verdandi tilted the bowl, and something black made a little puddle on the piece of paper. Verdandi then took a pendant from a necklace and pushed it into the black puddle.

A wax seal? I thought. *Ariel's great-grandfather was a little dramatic.*

She then signed her name. Ariel stood and walked to the front of the moot. Reaching across the large, stretched-out desk, Ariel took the paper and walked toward the exit, giving me the slightest nod, indicating I should follow. I rose and walked quickly from the room behind Ariel.

Ariel handed me the paper as we strode from the room, and I read from the stylized text to myself.

"It is hereby ordered by the council of Norns and the office of Vidar, whose seal below is affixed. That the life of *Marquis Zarov* is hereby forfeit by the laws of gods and man. The arrangers henceforth referred to as the organization herein entreat you to prosecute this order by any means necessary up to and including the death of the member(s) tasked with *Marquis Zarov's* elimination. All relevant data will be attached in the file behind this order of writ. Feather or heart, you will balance the scales."

I kept reading, but it turned into legalese.

— *Chapter 12* —

Hotel California

Ariel sat, typing furiously, treating her keyboard like it owed her money. "Fucking morons," she mumbled under her breath.

She looked up. "Your stuff has been moved down to the barracks on floor 20. You should head down there and get some sleep. You are going to get your ass kicked tomorrow."

"I'm tougher than I look."

She smiled wryly. "Have you secretly been working out like a tier-one operator for the last fifteen years without anyone finding out?"

"No, but...I work out."

She laughed out loud this time. "Sammi, please don't take this the wrong way. You are going to be pushed way past your limits over the next month, and even with all the best trainers and equipment money can buy, you will still be at a deficit to most opponents that are out there."

I didn't take offense, but I didn't feel like I was understanding her.

"So what you are saying is, I'm going to get killed no matter what?"

She shook her head. "No, but you don't understand what it means to be our enemy. Some of them, they are soft, weak, cooperate types that you could kill with a brick and a decent throwing arm. But the other type of enemies we face are different. They don't go home from the field. The only thing clean on them is their rifle. The only thing they understand is violence. Some of the ones from third-world countries have a third-grade reading level in their own language. The fight is all they know. They can survive on rice with maggots in it for years without ever noticing anything is wrong with their diet. They sleep in the dirt when the sun goes down because where else would they sleep? What I am trying to tell you is, if you don't throw yourself into this world with the same enthusiasm and need to understand as that generic enemy, you will fail."

I thought about this for several seconds before I responded, "I guess I can't fail then."

She smiled ruefully. "No, you can't."

I went to the elevator and pressed the button labeled 20. The elevator fell away under my feet, causing a moment of panic. I reflected on Ariel's words as the elevator descended. I felt resolve to continue this path. I felt the burden of expectation that Ariel, Doc, and the others had bestowed upon me. For the first time in my life, however, I had the missing component. I had the why.

My whys up till now had only been, make money and survive. Now I had a bright, burning purpose beneath my sternum.

The door opened onto a floor that looked like the lobby of a hotel. There was a front desk that looked like it had been plucked from a Holiday Inn, with a wizened man sitting behind it, a single computer monitor in front of him. Above his head was a large red neon sign that read in cursive script, "Hotel Californa." I smiled to myself.

The older man behind the desk noticed me. "You Sammi?"

I nodded. "Yes, sir."

He laughed. "Sir was my grandfather. Or whatever old fucks like me in denial are supposed to say."

The jovial, crochety man walked out from behind his desk and offered his hand. I shook it.

"Name is Denny. I am the quartermaster of this fine establishment. If you need anything while you are here, let me know. For right now, let's get you in bed. I hear you have an early morning tomorrow."

I pursed my lips, nodding in acknowledgment, partially dreading the suffering to come.

Arrangements by Ariel

Denny handed me a room key that had the number 69 on it. I knew instantly that this was either Doc or Ariel's doing.

He pointed down the hallway to the right.

"Your room is last one on the right. All your stuff is in there, clothes in the closet. Dial 0 on the phone if you need me for anything."

I took the key card. "Thank you, Denny."

I walked to my room and touched the key card to the door, and it popped open. Inside there were six beds, but none of them were occupied. I saw my clothes put neatly in the closet and my two pairs of shoes on the floor. I unlaced my boots and fell asleep before I was even in the bed.

— *Chapter 13* —

Good Fucking Morning

THE NEXT MORNING, A bang on the door jolted me awake. I shot out of the bed.

With an internal groan, I opened the door. Doc was standing there with a Cheshire grin on his face.

"Good fucking morning to you, sir." He handed me a microfiber shirt and gym shorts, saying, "First thing we are going to do is go on a run, and then we have an appointment with the lab and the armory. After that, your day is going to decrease in enjoyment immensely because we have combatives and then some classroom time from which you will have homework."

I nodded, taking the clothes and slipped them on. I put on my running shoes, and then Doc said, "Follow me."

We walked to the elevator. Doc pushed the button for floor 13. The elevator asked him for his key card. He scanned it, and it sank with, as always, startling speed.

The elevator opened on to an open floor that looked like a warehouse.

There was gym equipment on one half of the room; all of which was occupied by various fit and scary-looking individuals already into their morning routines. The other half was an open space with padded floors and walls, where various couplings of people rolled around on the ground, trying to strangle each other. Others stood and traded blows with MMA gloves.

Doc walked to the wall covered in high-end treadmills and spoke, "We will stretch then start with two miles of light jogging and then alternating sprinting and jogging for the next eight miles."

My heart caught in my throat. I had never run this far in my life, so I braced myself for the pain to come. I nodded and followed Doc through a series of stretches then stepped onto the treadmill.

Twenty minutes later, I was gasping for breath. It felt like I was suffocating, but I kept willing my legs forward as they started to go numb. All the events of the last week danced in my mind like angry little bumblebees, with one little bright firefly mixed in.

The whelming wave of emotions that were coursing through me made me reflect on B-Don and how wasteful and pointless his death was. In the same thought line, I considered that had he lived, I probably would not be doing what I am doing right now. I promised myself, screaming into my own soul, You *will not let his death mean nothing! No one may ever know, but that doesn't matter.*

My mind filled with thoughts of Ariel. I found my second wind and kept running. The suffering was all that existed as my mind went blank and quiet. I tried to keep pace with Doc but fell behind drastically.

The tempo of jog, sprint, jog was beginning to become dread, pain, dread. Doc stepped down from his treadmill. I still had just under a half mile to go. I kept pushing, refusing to give in to my body that was screaming, *Stop.*

The mile tracker crossed the tenth mile, and my feet felt like jelly. I stepped from the treadmill.

Doc looked like he had just casually walked across the room. Not like he just ran ten miles.

Doc nodded. "Not bad, buddy. You are slow as shit, but you don't give up. That is all that matters."

I was panting, but I nodded my response.

"Come on. Time to juice you up and get you fitted for your ronin."

I didn't speak because I still couldn't speak, but I walked behind Doc, and we went to the elevator. He pressed the button for floor 30.

— *Chapter 14* —

Southern Comfort

THE ELEVATOR SHOT UP and opened onto a floor that looked like the check inn counter at an ER.

"This is our R and D Lab, but when need requires, it also doubles as our trauma care center. No hospital visits for the world's most attractive assassins."

I laughed nervously. The bleach white walls and glass door gave the place a feel like you were walking into Umbrella Corporation headquarters.

There was a receptionist behind the desk. "Hey, Doc. Go on in."

He nodded to her. "Watcha doin' later?"

She smiled a devilish grin. "You probably."

He laughed. "My good woman, what do you take me for, a harlot?"

She laughed louder. "Um…yeah."

He shrugged. "Fair enough."

The door opened automatically, and we stepped into what looked like an advertisement for a university.

There were dogs being lead around on leashes and people milling around what looked like a state-of-the-art laboratory in casual clothes. It looked like Q's lab from *James Bond*. There were gadgets, gizmos, and mannequins everywhere—all with some form of tech being tried on them. People with lasers took measurements of some kind of gun in the corner.

There were flasks on hot plates and test tubes with flowers in them being cultivated and snipped.

People of what looked like every nationality were present, some talking and laughing; others stared hard at computer screens. One guy bounced a tennis ball off a wall.

There was a glass barrier at the back of the expanse that read, "Bio Containment Level 4. Authorized personnel only. Full PPE required."

Doc motioned toward a lowered area, a mini Greek colosseum, with people sitting and talking quietly. At the bottom of the mini theatre was a desk with what looked like ten monitors, all at various heights and angles.

"Good morning, Dr. Isley," Doc said.

A woman in her mid-forties stuck her head from around middle monitor. "If it isn't the cutest pain in my ass this organization has ever produced. How you doing, Doc?"

Her Southern draw took me by surprise.

"Dr. Isley, this is Sammi. I need you to juice him up and get him into fighting shape."

She looked at me with a dissecting gaze. "Hey there, Sammi. I'm Dr. Lillian Isley. Very nice to meet you."

She stepped from behind her desk and gave my hand a shake. Her clothing surprised me too. She had on Wrangler blue jeans, a flannel shirt, and cowboy boots.

"Very nice to meet you, ma'am. I mean Dr. Isley."

She smiled. "Ooh, I like him. Good manners and some humility. Where on God's forsaken wasteland of a planet did you find him?"

"In a bar," Doc said.

You could almost hear the sweet tea in her laugh. "Well, let's get to work. Follow me."

She walked quickly up the small staircase, back to the madhouse above. She walked over to a set of what looked like lethal injection tables and motioned for me to sit down. I hesitated, feeling a prickling fear about what was obviously an unknowable situation.

"Don't worry, buddy. If you are nice to her, she won't turn you into a newt or any other creature," Doc said, comforting me.

Dr. Isley laughed as she pulled over what looked like a very large toolbox.

"Okay, Sammi, just so you understand what we are doing here. The cocktail of drugs I am about to give you has one purpose—to make you a more lethal predator. Your muscles will no longer decay over time without usage. Your telomeres will no longer shorten with age, and your mitochondria in your blood cells will work at 200 percent efficiency. What we are about to do is going to change how you fight, how you train, and how you think about your own limitations."

My mind was swimming with questions, but the first one I blurted out was, "What is in this stuff?"

She said, "Well, part of it is BAM-15, a formerly experimental drug, and then we will hit you with a stem-cell therapy that is infused with a mild anabolic steroid and akimine. We will then get a blood panel and prescribe you a perfect balance of vitamins and supplements based on your levels. After that, you come see one of my techs once every three months to have everything redone."

My eyes were wide. "Holy shit," I said in awe.

"It's not polite to say naughty words in front of a lady, Sammi. Now lean back on the table, and hold the rest of your certainly endless questions for a more-appropriate fucking time."

I leaned back on the table. The doctor pulled out an IV kit and deftly had it into my arm in seconds. She connected it to an IV bag of what I assumed was saline. She then made an injection into my thigh muscle and another one into my shoulder muscle.

She then injected the IV bag with a green translucent substance and said, "There now, all done. Now all you have to do is be near Doc for the next half hour, wait for this bag here to be empty, and then you don't have to see me for a while."

I nodded and rolled my shoulder in pain. "Well, I will miss you, but your needles I could take or leave."

She smiled crookedly. "I am going to remind you that you didn't like my needles in about twenty minutes."

I cocked my head in confusion.

"Yeah, you are about to get a big rush of euphoria, and then you are going to feel what it's like to have an unfair advantage."

He was right. About fifteen minutes later, I felt a head rush and what felt like being high on a stimulant. I felt…good. The soreness and jellylike feeling from the treadmill earlier receded. I felt better than I had felt in my entire life. I could feel every neuron of my body like the volume on life just got turned up to eleven.

"Hey, Dr. Isley."

She looked up from a tablet and the blood-test kit she was preparing. "Yes, sweetie."

I smiled. "I lied earlier. I think I like you and your needles."

She giggled sarcastically. "Well, color me surprised."

── *Chapter 15* ──

100

After the head rush passed and Dr. Isley completed my blood test, Doc ushered me from the lab and into the elevator, certain that I was about to be exposed to a whole new, unfamiliar world. Like the last eight times this door opened and closed, I prepared myself to step into a giant room filled with giant guns and massive, brawny men, taking weapons apart for indiscernible reasons.

Doc pressed both the button that was marked with a simple B and the button for floor 1.

The electronic voice said, "Please scan key card."

Doc scanned his key card.

The voice answered again, "Please recite pass phrase."

Doc intoned, "Does an emerald lose its quality if it is not praised?"

The elevator beeped and sank quickly.

"Our armory is just above our underground motor pool and, in contrast with the lab, not nearly used as often. We need tech way more than we need guns around here. Even though your last few days may make that hard to believe."

I nodded in understanding. "But we still need guns, right?"

Doc gave a half smile. "We need guns, lots of guns."

The door slid open before I could compliment him on the reference.

I stepped into a room filled with nothing, just a bunch of empty workbenches and a sealed cage at the other end of the room.

A single small-framed man stepped from the cage's side door.

"Hey there, Doc. How's it hanging?"

Doc smiled, giving the man a backslapping hug. "A little to the left today, but nothing a cold shower won't fix."

The small man's loud laugh echoed in the empty space.

"Sammi, this is Edwin. Edwin, Sammi."

I offered the man my hand, and he shook it.

"Very nice to meet you, Sammi. Here to get your Superman costume?"

I smiled, uncertain. "I think so, but can we leave the blue and red out. Not really my colors."

The man smirked. "I used to be able to make our armor customized to each operator, but then someone came along and ruined my fun."

Doc hung his head in shame. "It was me. I ruined the fun."

"What did you do that could have possibly gotten Edwin's fun ruined?"

Doc recounted the tale. "Well, like Edwin said, he would customize to any spec I gave. But when Ariel saw the back of my level 4 composite armor that costs fifty thousand dollars a set, cera-coated with naked anime girls, she banned all but the simplest customizations and made Edwin here cera-coat every set of armor just to make sure he and everyone else hated me. A lot. Some of them are still mad at me."

I ugly laughed and managed to get out, "Over naked anime girls?"

"Well, the large cocks that were turned into a coat of arms on the chest plate probably didn't hurt either."

I laughed even harder, with tears coming.

Edwin shook his head. "I thought it was funny too until Ariel saw it, and she has been taking her revenge on Doc and I ever since. Anyway, lets head to our Mocap room."

I shrugged. "Let's go. Wait a second, Doc. You said the chest plate had a coat of arms. What was the name on the coat of arms?"

Doc giggled. "Shaft."

Edwin smiled as we walked. Looking over his shoulder, he said, "That part was my idea."

We went to the other side of the room, where there was a set of double doors. Edwin stepped through first, and there was a long hallway. On one side, thick glass windows looked out onto a small shooting range. Two men and a woman moved together through shooting drills in full kit.

They drew my eye for a moment, but then Edwin took a right, opening a small door.

We stepped inside. It was an empty room with green walls, ceiling, and floor. There were lights in the corners of the room and several alien-looking pieces of tech.

"Okay, get naked, Sammi, and put on that green jumpsuit with the little black balls on it," Edwin recited as he played with various gizmos.

I complied and put on the jumpsuit, wondering what this was for. A memory dredged up from my childhood. The making of *Halo 3* miniseries. People running around and jumping in suits that looked just like this. Warm feelings of nostalgia coursed briefly through me.

The suit felt like wearing nothing. Edwin stepped over with what looked like three black Hula-Hoops suspended on three levels by long bars of metal. He picked up the frame and slid it over my head.

Edwin clarified, "Hi-res laser scan. This will give us your bodies exact fit, and we will make your armor and helmet based off this scan."

A second or two later, he removed the Hula-Hoops and frame. Edwin pushed everything else to the corner of the room.

"Okay, now, Sammi, jog in place."

I complied.

He said, "Stop. Now do shuttle runs, back and forth."

I did as I was instructed.

"Okay, bend down and touch your toes."

I did so, saying, "Is the next part where I drop it like it's hot?"

Edin laughed himself almost to tears, and then he looked at the celling for a moment in thought. "Alright, Sammi, that's almost everything we need."

Edwin looked at Doc. "You want me to, or do you want to?"

Doc smiled. "I've got it."

Doc rolled his shoulders and stepped from the corner.

"Alright, buddy, so here is the plan. I'm going to come over there and beat the shit out of you. You are going to try and stop me."

My heart instantly jumped into my throat, pulse pounding the preamble to pain.

"O…okay," I stammered.

In far less than a second, Doc closed the distance and slammed into me, knocking the breath from my lungs.

I didn't fight the fall; I rolled with it. Doc ended up on my face for a second, but I slipped my head free and scrambled back toward him, wrapping my arms around his waist. Doc playfully slapped my head just to let me know, if this was real, I would probably be unconscious already.

I postured up and tried to pin Doc's arms to his side. He laughed, falling onto his back. His legs locked around my neck in what I knew was called a triangle choke. I refused to tap, remembering what Ariel said, "No matter what happens, don't give up." All thought faded, and there was nothing.

"There he is."

I woke, looking at a green ceiling, with Doc and Edwin standing over me.

Doc smiled down at me.

"That was so fucking hard, buddy. I don't think I have ever seen someone go voluntarily unconscious in one of these. Most people tap."

I coughed lightly, feeling much better, but with a small headache.

"Well, Ariel told me not to quit. That felt like quitting."

The looked at each other and started laughing hysterically. They were crying by the time I got out.

"What? I don't get it."

Doc wiped a tear and said, "Buddy, you are so fucking whipped. *Django Unchained* called and wants its schtick back."

Edwin said, "You are so whipped Ariel has custom-made pockets in her purses for your balls."

Doc heaved. "You are so goddamn whipped God himself has put out a warrant on Ariel for domestic-violence charges."

I raised my hands in surrender. "Yes, yes, I get it. I'm whipped. No shame in admitting that from the now-unemployed former bartender."

They made calming gestures more to themselves than me. I stood up.

"Alright, that was…fun? What's next."

Edwin walked over. "Need you to get naked again."

"Edwin, you can just ask me out if you want otherwise. I'm going to start charging you."

They giggled like five-years-olds. Through their silly fits, Edwin got out.

"Need the suit back."

I got undressed and redressed in my workout clothes.

Doc clapped his hands together. "Okay, we have a meeting with Patton for combatives. You'll meet the rest of your training group there."

We got into the elevator after saying goodbye to Edwin.

Doc pressed the button for floor 13. The gym was completely empty, except for a group of about twenty people all standing and talking on the mats on the other half of the room.

Doc said, "Go introduce yourself to the jacked, old guy. You belong to him and his friends for the next three hours. After that, head to the Norn moot for schooltime."

"See you later?"

Doc shook his head. "Probably not. Dagger has a meeting and then training. I will see you tomorrow."

I walked over to the group, and there was a short but incredibly dense man in his late sixties standing off to the side of the crowd, with two other men that looked like Greek gods.

"Hello, sir, I'm Sammi."

He said plainly, "Why the fuck should I care? Get in line."

Not seeing a line, I shrugged to myself and joined the crowd of people.

"Everyone, shut the fuck up!" the old man shouted.

Up the fuck everyone shut and silently stared at the old man. "School circle."

Everyone but me seemed to know what that meant and either sat kneeled or stood, so I stood at the edge of the semicircle of humans. The two giant men flanked either side of the old man.

"My name is Henry Sheffield. This is the first and last time you will hear that name because everyone here calls me Paton. Now, you all were something else before coming here. Most of you were soldiers, criminals, or both. Not anymore. There is only one standard by which you will now be measured—mine. To understand my standard, listen closely. Approximately seven hundred and fifty years before Christ was born was a man named Heraclitus. He was in the business of training warriors. As now am I. Here are his words. 'Out of every one hundred men they send me, eighty of them are nothing but targets. Ten of 'em shouldn't even be here. Nine of them are real fighters. Ah, but one, one of them is a warrior, and I must find him because he will bring the others home.'"

Everyone was silent still and barely breathing. You could have heard a mote of dust hit the floor.

"So just show me that you have a discipline problem. Show me that you are a quitter. Show me any of these qualities, and we will shitcan you so fast that your ancestors will get whiplash. Anybody that doesn't wish to proceed should leave now!"

No one moved.

The old man continued, much quieter this time, "Alright then, your instructors will guide you through the first set of drills."

The minutes crawled by. Push-ups, sit-ups, jumping jacks, low crawling, sprints. The pain sat in and never left. The exhaustion set in and never seemed to go away. There it was, the stuff Dr. Isley pumped into me made me never fall to full exhaustion. I knew this would only compound over time.

We learned arm bars, kimura locks, Americanas, Darce chokes, the rear naked choke, and bulldog chokes. We wrestled each other, and sometimes it was a two on one or a three on one. They then introduced Tasers to the mix. I was tased until my balls hurt. Then I got tased in the balls. I couldn't take any more. But I realized that

I could not quit either. On and on it went, with no sense of time. I stumbled from drill to drill in a daze.

Finally, Paton called, "Stop. That's our time for today. Everyone, hit the showers and then get to class. Same time here tomorrow. After I whip you green, disgusting, street creatures into something resembling people, we will be sending you out for a monthlong tactical training, then you might even become useful people."

We all were laying on the mats, gross and tired. A small-framed, beautiful, young lady was sitting next to me, and she made eye contact with me.

"Hey there, champ, what's your name?"

Her Australian accent gave a staccato, machine-gun-like tempo to her speech. Her looks didn't hurt the confused response I gave.

"S-Sammi."

She giggled. "Sammi, you this smooth with all the ladies, or am I special?"

I laughed nervously. "I am definitely this smooth all of the time. You are not special. I mean I am sure you are a special person... But. Never mind."

She kicked me gently in the arm. "You aren't doing too bad so far. What are you doing after classroom time tonight?"

I realized that she had just asked me out. All the alarm bells in my brain said, *Run, little dumbass, run.*

"I think I will be passing out after the day I have had."

She nuzzled up close to me. "Sure you can't stay up just a little later than normal for...extracurriculars?"

I pulled away. "No, sorry. I have a girlfriend, and she would literally, in every sense of the word, kill me if I did that."

She frowned. "Too bad. Well, if you change your mind, my name's Cindi, and I am in room 44 in the HC."

"What?"

She shook her head. "You must have just got here. HC, Hotel California."

I nodded in understanding. "Oh, acronym, got it. Nice to meet you, Cindi."

I stood and fast-walked. My muscles were protesting, but I pushed toward the elevators and headed for my room. I put the Aussie girl as far from my thoughts as humanly possible.

— Chapter 16 —

Aldrich

THE MORNING CHURCH SERVICE provided some relief from the hot, humid, rainy Venezuelan climate. Aldrich listened as the pastor recounted the trial of Saint Paul in beautiful Spanish prose.

Aldrich smiled, checking his watch first then his phone. Right on time.

The sermon came to an end, and Aldrich walked into the bustling Sunday streets of Caracas.

A man wearing a rough-looking blue suit sat at an outside bistro; his coffee had just arrived.

Aldrich looked up and down the street. Seeing one of his security details and seeing that he wasn't giving him any warning signs, he went to the man's table and sat.

"Mr. Zarov, why did you need to meet me in person so urgently? Surely, Edward was going to bring you to our meeting next month?"

"Edward is dead."

Aldrich closed his eyes and said a prayer for his fallen friend. "God's ways are higher than ours, Mr. Zarov. It was his time."

Zarov shook his head fiercely. "God had nothing to do with it." Zarov reached into his jacket and pulled a file folder out and handed it to the older Eastern European man.

"What is this now?" Aldrich picked up the folder and read. "And you didn't call me? How stupid can you be, Marquis? Please, that is not rhetorical. Tell me, if you don't mind, how far down the incompetence spiral were you prepared to go before calling me?"

Zarov winced at the rebuke. "I tried to clean up the situation myself, but it was not a simple matter as you can see. Things got... messy."

Aldrich stretched and ordered a coffee from the waitress.

"Lord, give me strength. Are Galo's assets secure?"

Zarov nodded. "I drained everything into my own accounts in Monaco. On that front, at least we are clean."

Aldrich sighed, relaxing somewhat. "Zarov, you are now Mr. Gallo's replacement. Please understand me when I say, this is probationary until I state otherwise."

Zarov nodded in understanding. "I am up to date on most projects Edward was working on. I will put together a list of what I know."

Aldrich smiled. "That would be wise. One you probably didn't know about because it did not require bloodshed was the Nigerian mining contract. I will get you a file and a plane ticket. This is already overdue."

Zarov leaned forward and said quietly, "What about the bartender and his bitch?"

Aldrich scowled. "Language. That bartender and his so-called bitch managed to kill your interdiction team, and then...they killed your hit team when information was no longer your goal. You tried to appease me, Marquis. I trust that will be the last time you do that. Yes?"

Zarov felt cold fingers of terror run up his spine. "Yes."

Aldrich nodded gravely. "Good. I'll work on building a target package on this variable. You will go to Nigeria and get the president to sign that fucking contract."

Zarov nodded his head respectfully. "On the way, sir."

Aldrich dismissed the man with a wave of his hand.

Finishing his coffee, he mused to himself, "We are almost there, only a few more pieces to the puzzle. God, give me the strength to do what your children have been apologizing for."

— *Chapter 17* —

The Lady and the Tiger

I RETURNED TO MY room and checked my phone. There was one text message unread. It was from Ariel: *Hey, babe, on your way to class stop by my office I have a surprise for you. <3 Xoxo*

I got in the shower and quickly scrubbed the grime from my body, put on clothes, and nearly ran to the elevator.

I loved her. I didn't give a shit anymore. She was the only thing in the world that made me get out of bed in the morning. Every time I was with her, I had to downplay how I was feeling because I didn't want her to feel like I was clingy or moving too fast, or give her any of the million other reasons why girls stop liking you.

This elevator opened in the middle of the office. Unlike the ornate lobby, this one opened into a hallway. I fast-walked, but slowed my pace when I made the last turn, purposely slowing down. I pushed open the giant oak doors and stepped into the lair of Ariel.

She was sitting at her desk, sharpening a long dagger on a series of wet stones. She looked up when I walked in. She put the knife down almost reverently.

She stood and walked toward me, a wry smile on her face. My face, I hoped, betrayed nothing. We met in the middle of the room, and she gently took my face in her hands and kissed me deep, and the kissing turned into making out. For several minutes, we stayed like that. Finally, she pulled away.

"Good job today not giving up. Only a lifetime to go. Ready for your surprise.?"

I kissed her neck. Her body tensed with appreciation and then relaxed.

Stopping, I said, "You are the only surprise I will ever need."

She giggled sweetly. "Later. Come sit."

Knowing she needed me to be in business mode now, I stopped and complied. She sat in her chair, and the massive screen in the wall to the left flicked on and showed a picture of the one man that could take me out of the mood I had just been in.

"We found Zarov in Venezuela this morning. He appears to be lying low. Very low now. He ditched his cell yesterday after the attack on us went sideways. This was picked up at the airport in Caraccas. We have a team on him now. Our best intel says that he will be hiding in Caracas for the foreseeable future. With that in mind, I have a little influence, as you know, on exactly how the orders from the moot are carried out. So we are going to wait and sit on Zarov until your training is completed."

I nodded and said, "If you need to take him out sooner than later, I understand."

Ariel smiled, accepting my agreeableness for what it was—an understanding of reality.

"Well, being my boyfriend has to have some perks."

I stood and walked around her desk. Leaning down, I kissed her and slid down to her neck.

"Don't you have class?"

I groaned. "Yes… Fuck."

"I may head down to the barracks later if you are very lucky."

I sauntered toward the exit and spoke, "Well, you know me. I am made of luck."

Looking back up at Zarov, I felt the prickling fear and the void-like sadness that I felt the night he took B-Don from the world, and said quietly to myself as I walked from the room, "See you soon."

— *Chapter 19* —

The Geriatric in Tie-Dye

I walked to the Norn moot, and the false wall opened. Twenty or so students that were in our combatives class were clustered around the front of the room.

I recognized the old man at the podium as Skuld. He was wearing a multicolored suit that looked like it had been tie-dyed and then color-coordinated by someone that was color-blind.

The suit almost made me laugh out loud, and it seemed that my classmates were likewise amused. I sat on the row closest to the front.

Skuld tapped the mic and said, "Can everyone hear me without this thing?"

Everyone nodded. He walked to the front of the stage and sat down on the edge, eye to eye with us.

"You probably think you are all here to learn how to be better killers, right? Learn some supersecret, tactical, cool-guy stuff. But you are here to learn the why, not the how. More important than knowing when to kill is knowing when not to. Because understanding the aftereffects of a killing is one of the hardest pieces of math you can contemplate. As an example, who here thinks my outfit is super-expensive designer clothing?"

About four hands went up.

"And who thinks that this crazy, geriatric patient just took a suit and slung some paint on it?"

Some laughs floated through the room. Five hands went up.

"And who thinks it is an object lesson about putting thoughts into people's heads?"

The rest of the hands in the room went up.

"Most of you think this is probably the right answer, and in a way, it is right, but in another way, it's wrong. The full answer is this, I know that wearing a ridiculous, silly suit will immediately focus your attention on me and make thoughts about me and the suit enter your mind with little to no effort on my part. Without a word spoken by me, I gained your undivided attention. I have subverted your doxastic closure. I am literally living in your heads rent free. Remember, putting thoughts in the heads of the unwilling is the territory of the predator. You have to learn to think like one if you want to succeed."

A newfound respect for the man in front of them seemed to propagate through the group.

Skuld continued, "If you are willing to die for us, you should know a little about how we started. This firm was founded by a man named Gregory Vidar, the adopted son of British immigrants and the second-in-command of the OSS during World War II. Second only to Wild Bill Donovan. He had an idea, one that would help shape the future. His idea was this. What if Hitler never existed? What if, when Hitler was a baby, someone from the future showed up and killed him in his crib? Would things have turned out differently? He got a degree from Oxford before the war in philosophy and tried many times to answer this question during and after. The answer that he came to was this. If Hitler never existed, things would have turned out differently, but constant vigilance would be required full-time to monitor the global situation and continuously put down threats to humanity. Because the thing that allows Hitler to exist is not some overarching willpower or natural talent for public speaking."

Skuld tapped a button on his laptop, and pictures of dictators throughout history scrolled on the screen.

"There is no secret formula to becoming a dictator or a tyrant or a mass murderer. The thing we are fighting against in the shadows is nothing short of human nature itself. The need to belong to something greater than yourself, i.e., tribalism. The greatest force for good and evil on this planet. The servile, worshipful masses are by their very nature in the habit of elevating people that are sometimes the worst choices possible to the pinnacles of power. All it takes to change the world is one good lie and a river of blood."

One of the younger recruits raised his hand and said, "Did you just quote Captain Price from *Call of Duty*?"

Laughter echoed in the near-empty chamber.

"I did indeed. Great guy, that Captain Price. My second favorite quote is, someone has to make the bad guys scared of the dark."

Another round of laughter bounced through the small gathering.

"While dictators may be one problem, the main problem now is this."

A mushroom cloud appeared on the screen.

"We will give you some reading on proliferation as a concept, but the main takeaway is this. Take the number of apocalyptic psychopaths in the world and then think about the number of ways we can end our species. Bioweapons. Dirty bombs. Nukes. Both the number of individuals and methods increase every year. We make sure they never exist together. Now our scope of targets has expanded. We also target mass murders, or people that are aspiring mass murderers."

He then clicked a remote, and three images appeared on the screen. One woman and two men. Silence returned to the room.

"I need a vote. The woman on the left has been spending a lot of time on anti-government websites and has become radicalized by an anarchist sect that wants to destroy all world governments. The man in the center is a mercenary that works in the Democratic Republic of the Congo for the highest bidder. Nothing that is included in the intelligence report has been marked as an outlier. The man on the right is a Silicon Valley executive that has been keeping child-labor laws suppressed in Nigeria, where his cobalt mines sacrifice approximately five children a day to make iPhones. Questions?"

I raised my hand. Skuld pointed to me.

"You told us what the two men do for a living. What does the woman do?"

Skuld smiled. "Excellent question. Twenty points to Gryffindor. She is a lieutenant commander in the Air Force currently in control of a nuclear missile silo in Nebraska."

Exclamations started flowing between my classmates.

"Who wants to kill the woman?"
Almost all the hands in the room went up.
"And the mercenary?"
My hand went up with a few others.
"And the Silicon Valley Executive."
Two hands went up. Skuld nodded.
"Okay, so let's see how your choices worked out. You all chose to kill the radical. So your direct-action team went in and killed her in her sleep. They made the whole situation look like a home invasion. She was a mother of two, and her nine-year-old son watched you do the deed. Ten years later, that son gets radicalized by another group online called ISIS. He travels to northern Iraq and joins in the fight against the Americans and Kurds. His command of the English language helps recruiting efforts and draws thousands of foreign fighters to the conflict, prolonging it for a year. Thousands of people are dead because of the emotional trauma you subjected this young man to. Did you make the right call?"

Everyone started talking among themselves for a minute.

Skuld interjected, "Anyone have an answer?"

Cindi put her hand up. "It was the wrong decision. If we would have left her alone and put the right word in the right person's ear, she could have been made irrelevant with a phone call. Thus, not allowing the son to have the trauma needed to be vulnerable."

"Very good, but what if she would have launched nukes or gotten a few stolen by her comrades online? Would that not have created a worse situation?"

I raised my hand. Skuld nodded.

"She did not have the skill set or understanding of how to steal the nukes. They taught her how to fire them with a team, not how to fire them or steal them on her own."

Skuld nodded appreciatively.

"Very good. While it is possible, she acquired the skill needed on her own that is unlikely. Now, what about our other two contestants on the kill is right?"

The mercenary's picture was highlighted.

"All three of these subjects were terminated by us in real life. The man in the middle ended up with the highest body count by far. We knew he had allies in the Hutu tribe in Rwanda in the early nineties. We knew that he was probably about to sell them a ridiculous amount of firepower. We killed him, but a week too late. A year later, the weapons he helped them procure were turned on the Tutsi minorities. Eight hundred thousand people died in the genocide. They would not have been so efficient in the killing if this man would not have supplied them with massive amounts of AK-47s and grenades. So the small cost of killing him had the potential to save hundreds of thousands of lives. But we were just a little too late."

Skuld highlighted the mercenary on the screen. "Any questions about mean, old Mr. Merc?"

No one spoke.

"Good. Onto Silicone valley man. We took him out and a few of his Chinese friends, and we took out a few key government officials that were being bribed for the mining rights. Result, two years later, there are child-labor laws in Nigeria that have stopped what was basically slavery. They now have control of the resource, and the country's GDP grew by a factor of three. Which of these was the most successful?"

A small man two seats down from me said, "The Silicon Valley executive was the most successful, but only because there was a follow-on plan that led to that success."

Skuld nodded. "Very good. Most of our greatest successes required more than one death. So one was unwarranted, one was too late, and one was successful. Why did we only get a thirty-three on the test?"

Another person in the front row spoke, "Information, specifically the processing of the information."

Skuld nodded. "Very good. Our success rate up until 2010 was around 50 percent. After it has been far closer to 85 percent. The only thing that changed was, the amount of information we are able to gather has increased one thousandfold thanks to the Internet. In your rooms when you get back tonight will be three folders. In each of these folders will be a name and a profile much like the ones here today. You will read and internalize everything in these folders, and you will choose to kill one person. We will then review your choices and see how you did. That's all for today. Go get some food and rest up. You are going to need it."

I stood, and on the way out the door, Cindi gave me a smirk and bumped into me playfully. "Excuse me, clumsy."

I didn't bite. "No problem. Have an excellent evening."

— Chapter 16 —

I Need a Weapon

Ariel laid lazily on my barrack's bunk bed, not wearing a single piece of clothing.

"That won't work. If you kill the college professor, the outpouring of support for her ideals will only calcify the people she has already ensnared in her position."

"Well, who then? The seventeen-year-old just has a fucked-up sense of humor and an obsession with guns, and the nonprofit president just got caught up with people that were no good, and there is nothing in here to indicate he is going to do anything worse than a speeding ticket ever again."

She sighed. "Well, have another look at everyone's messaging history. Is there anything there?"

I took a few minutes and reread the history. Then I saw it, a gap in time between messages for the seventeen-year-old, a monthlong gap.

"The gap?"

Ariel nodded. "Very good."

I shook my head again. "Well, that still isn't enough for the moot. What else am I missing?"

"Who said you were missing something?"

I thought, and my mind strayed to another subject. "There is a girl in my class who has hit on me twice since I got there."

Ariel's eyes did not betray anything. "Oh yeah, which one?"

She said it so matter-of-factly I was immediately suspicious and careful with my response. "Well, that depends. Are you going to kill her?"

Ariel laughed, full and bright. "No, Sammi, I will not kill your would-be mistress. Besides, monogamy is so two thousand and late."

I was now very confused. "What do you mean?"

She rolled over onto her elbows.

"Monogamy in the long run is destined to fail for about 60 percent of people our age. We move too fast, our interests are too varied, and our wants, needs, and desires change by the day most of the time. Expecting two people that want to fuck each other not to fuck is the very opposite of what nature built us for. And using sociological trauma to enforce that medieval mindset is silly."

I was more confused. "Are you saying we are in an open relationship or…"

"As long as it is comfortable for you, yes. I don't currently need, desire, or have time for anyone else. My emotional well-being is in your hands. But I really could care less what you do with your body. It is your mind and soul that belongs to me. Not your body."

I nodded. "I don't really have any interest in anyone else either."

Her green eyes tore deep into my being. "Well, I am a hard act to follow. But maybe you will be disappointed with our next tumble through the sheets. Only one way to find out."

In the middle of the night, Ariel slipped out of the room, barely waking me from my stupor.

At 6:00 a.m., my alarm went off, and a loud knock banged on my door. Groaning, I slid on my microfiber workout attire and opened the door, bracing for the pain to come.

Edwin and Doc stood there, looking like they had just drawn on the walls with crayons.

Doc had an iPad in his hands, and Edwin had a ronin helmet with the full suit of armor draped over his left shoulder.

Doc said, "So we might have done something that we are not supposed to do, and we want to show off."

I shook my head, still half asleep. "Okay, I guess. What did you do?" I yawned.

"Try your helmet on. And I think you are going to see very quickly why we are excited."

I took the helmet from Edwin's near-shaking arms.

Edwin guided me. "Just slide it on, and it will automatically seal in place."

I slid the helmet on and was surprised as its molded interior fit my head like it was hardly there at all. Once it was in place, it whirred a little mechanical buzz and snaped flush against my neck. The display in the helmet came up, and I recognized the tech that was exactly like the augmented reality from Ariel's Rolls-Royce.

The world washed into a brilliant and clear focus, and I was surprised that the field of vision was not narrow or tubelike. It was a full view of the world in front of me, with distances estimated and cover and concealment labeled on each surface. There was a mini map in the bottom right-hand corner.

As I was noticing the features, a voice broke across the speakers by my ears.

"What up, Sammi? My name is HITA. I'mma be your AI companion for all future gangsta activities."

"You guys did not put Snoop Dog in my helmet."

They smiled like five-year olds that had just invaded cookiestan.

Before Edwin could speak, Snoop, I mean HITA, spoke over my helmet and the iPad based on Doc's reaction.

"Bitch, what? I know you aren't coming at me sideways right now. If you steppin', then step little ass mufuka. My name is Hyper-Intuitive Tactical Artificial Intelligence. You can call me HITA. Unlike a tribe called Quest or a pimp named Slickback, you don't have to say the whole thing every time. Now, are we gonna have a problem?"

I quickly answered, "No, HITA, no problem from me. Happy to have you along."

"That's what the fuck I thought."

They were both trying their best to contain their laughter.

Edwin piped in, "It's not all for show. When shit gets real, HITA is programed to go all business mode. This will be standard issue by end of the day tomorrow for all ronin helmets. The AI, I mean, not Snoop Dog, but yours we gave a little something special because you gave me the idea on accident yesterday."

I was confused. "I don't know how I did that, but I'll take it."

Arrangements by Ariel

"Damn right, you'll take it. I am the shit," HITA tersely stated over the helmet's intercom.

Doc and Edwin were trying not to fall over laughing. Doc and Edwin instantly became serious.

Doc stated, almost begging, "Please don't tell Ariel."

Edwin echoed, "Oh my god, please, yes, do not tell Ariel. She will make yours like everyone else's. And then punish us in some unforeseen, terrible way."

I smiled, knowing they were right. "I won't tell Ariel. But I can't promise she won't find out on her own."

They nodded in silent resignation.

"How do I take this thing off?"

HITA replied, "Shit, all you had to do was ask. I was tired of having your dandruff-havin' ass head in here anyway."

The seal clicked open. I took the helmet off. I had a thought.

Putting the helmet back on, I asked HITA, "Can you make my voice sound different?"

HITA said, "Hell yeah. Different how though?"

I said, "Like Master Chief from the *Halo* games?"

HITA's laugh warbled and said, "Yeah, but I ain't Cortana, so keep that in mind."

I looked and Doc and Edwin, who looked confused, then I spoke, but Master Chief's voice came out, "Hey, Doc, I need a weapon."

Doc laughed. "I'd say, right this way, but your tactical training doesn't start for another week."

I nodded and said, "Helmet off."

HITA didn't speak, but the seals disengaged, and I slid the helmet off again.

Doc rubbed the sides of his mohawk. "Time to run."

My head drooped, anticipating the ten miles Doc was about to subject me to.

Surprisingly, we did cardio with the whole class this time. Then it was straight to the mats for combatives. After I had my clothes involuntarily folded with me still inside them, we broke to shower and eat. Then it was time to subject ourselves once again to the education of the Norns.

— *Chapter 17* —

Shoot, Don't Shoot

WE FILED INTO THE Norn moot for our daily education. Urd was at the front of the room, waiting on us, standing like an ancient, birdlike scion of a bygone age. We all carried our file folders that were left in our room from the previous evening.

"Good afternoon to all. My name is Urd. I am one of the three Norns that hold the strings of fate for this organization's victims. You may all be asking yourself why I phrase it this way. Because that is exactly what they are. Most of them are caught up in a game that they can't fully understand. Trapped either by Maslow's hierarchy of needs or by their own subjectivity. What I want you to learn today is not when to shoot but when not to. In my younger years, I was in favor of killing Nazis in their cribs. The mindset of the utilitarian was incredibly attractive, but as I have aged, what I have learned is that killing is never a solution. Simply a continuance of the problem. In your folders today are three potential victims. Out of those three, you will only select one that you think is worthy of death. The first is a seventeen-year-old named James. Now, James is a deeply troubled youth whose homelife resembles your average episode of *Jerry Springer*. But of note, James's social media indicates he fits the pattern of a school shooter. Yes, Cindi?"

Cindi stood and spoke with confidence, "Why would a potential school shooter be on our radar? He doesn't fit the directive."

Urd smiled broadly. "A fair question. The answer is complicated, but I will put it simply. Most school shooters are incompetent young men that have little to no chance of causing harm on a level high enough for us to intervene. If you look deeper into this young man's file, you will see that his family has sent him to a school where many children from this country's elite attend. This could have the potential to be geopolitically catastrophic, opening humanity to the possible death of millions."

Cindi nodded and sat down.

"The next man is the president of a nonprofit. He is forty-nine years old. His name is Daren, and he has a beautiful family. In 2008 Daren brokered a deal between the Iranian government and Bashar al-Assad. The deal was for two truckloads of sarin gas, which Bashar al-Assad then turned on his own people during the Syrian civil war several years later. Mitigating circumstances exist here. Signals intelligence indicates that he did so against his will and under duress. The final potential victim is a facilitator of human trafficking in Montenegro. His name is Vasili. Vasili helps hold together the peace between multiple large gangs that hold control of different parts of the country. Without Vasili, it is very likely that the region would fall into chaos for several years. Now, with that summary in mind, I am sure you all read the intelligence briefing on these three last night. So among yourselves now, you will give your reasons for or against the killing of these three. Let's start with James. Who wants to kill James?"

About five hands shot up, but mine stayed down. I thought I had the answer to this whole thing but wanted to wait to see if anything disproved my position. Cindi raised her hand for the seventeen-year-old.

Urd said, "Let's start with you."

Cindi stood. "We should kill the seventeen-year-old for several reasons. Preventing a school shooting would prevent the political and economic fallout that comes from such an event. With the new information that I did not see, the unintended consequence of having the children of high-powered individuals hurt, maimed, or killed could be irreparable. The obvious final reason is to prevent the suffering of the innocents at the school he may target."

Urd nodded and said, "Anyone want to disagree?"

Another student next to Cindi raised his hand. Urd pointed to him.

"We shouldn't kill James because, in the signals intelligence, there is nothing to indicate that he is an immediate and proximate threat to anyone. The kid is depressed, isolated, and mentally unstable. He needs therapy and some medication, not a bullet."

Urd nodded and spoke, "Okay, so James needs a doctor, not a bullet. Anyone else have anything to add?"

This continued for several minutes, everyone giving their well-founded positions based on statements made by philosophers past and present.

Finally, Urd said, "Young man, I don't think we have heard a word out of you yet."

It took me a few seconds to realize that everyone in the room was staring directly at me. I cleared my throat and stood up.

"We shouldn't kill any of them."

Everyone looked at me, puzzled, everyone, that is, except for Urd.

She smiled and said, "Go on."

"These pattern of life profiles are incomplete. They almost seem like they were purposefully left that way. There are massive gaps in the signals intelligence, where in James's case, we are missing two months of his communication. There are huge gaps in Daren's profile as well. There wasn't even a home address listed. How can we have enough information on a man to kill him when we don't even know where he calls home. If I had to choose, I would choose none of them. I would recommend that we gather more intel and wait."

I sat down.

Urd sighed. "You know, that cute little florist is going to be the death of me one day."

I smiled a knowing smile back at her.

Urd turned to the rest of the class. "Who here thinks Sammi got it right?"

Most of the hands went up, except Cindi's and a few others.

Urd said, "Young lady, do you think Sammi is wrong?"

Cindi stood up. "He is, wrong, I mean. He is assuming that we will have enough time to gather more intel. When could the school shooter do his deed? There is no guarantee that we get there on time as it currently stands, but we are supposed to wait?"

"Sammi?" Urd said.

I stood and replied, "Yes, posting pictures of guns on social media with captions like, 'I'm fixing to be famous,' is a red flag. Yes, he is deeply disturbed. But if you look at the time between our last intercepts, the kid could have gone to college early, and maybe now he is recovering because he isn't in the house anymore. Or five thousand other things could have happened in that time. We don't know, and if we don't know, we should be still."

Small side conversations started to break out, but Urd returned it to center. "Does anyone want to know who is right?"

Silence returned to the chamber.

"It is a very simple solution. Look at how much data you have. Is it comprehensive? Sammi has pointed out that it is not. Until you have identified your target, for all the former service members in the room, are you allowed to shoot?"

A chorus of headshakes and nos flowed toward Urd.

"That is correct, so in this 'shoot, don't shoot' exercise, what was the right answer?"

The room echoed, "Don't shoot."

Urd nodded. "In my opinion, that is always the correct answer, but my job here is to keep the immense power that we wield in check. I am always your opposition. When you want to hunt someone down, I am formulating arguments to stop you. Because that is my mission. Please don't believe that I think poorly of any of you because of this. But rather know that for you to have integrity in your purpose, I must do my job and do it well. That is all for today. Please gather your things, and the rest of the day is yours. Thank you for your attention."

We all started heading for the door, but Cindi wouldn't make eye contact with me. As we walked toward the exit, I said, "Hey, Cindi."

She turned an icy stare on me. "Were you trying to make me look bad?"

I was shocked. "Um, no, absolutely not."

Her expression softened, but only just. "Well, you could have fooled me. Sandbagging us all like that was not cool."

"All I said was the conclusion I came to."

She shook her head. "Sammi, you don't get it, do you? How you do in the Norn moot is what determines where you get posted in this company. Do poorly, and you get put on a security detail or posted in some remote region where they need you once every ten years."

I shook my head. "That can't be true. Ariel would have told m—"

I realized that I had just used Ariel's name in a place that I probably shouldn't have. Cindi's eyes bulged in their sockets.

"You don't mean…Vidar? Ariel Vidar is your girlfriend?"

I froze and stood perfectly still, waiting for lightning to strike me or a sniper's bullet to come through an air vent.

"Yes, Ariel is my girlfriend. So what?"

Cindi shook her head and fast-walked away from me.

"Whoa, whoa, whoa. What's the issue?"

She stopped abruptly. "The issue is, you are getting coaching from the top assassin on planet Earth. You have inside information on everything. Sammi, do you have any idea who you are in bed with?"

I squinted my eyes and said, "What do you mean?"

Cindi blew out a breath. "You don't even know how the Vidar is chosen, do you?"

I shook my head again in massive frustration. "Sure, Ariel is the great-granddaughter of the founder."

She grabbed my arm and sat me down in a chair against the back wall.

"Sammi, when the Vidar turns thirty, they go through the juvenile-detention records across the world and select the most violent and the most sociopathic kids that they can find. They then put the top five through a battery of tests that measure intelligence, reaction time, efficiency, pattern recognition, teachability. The winner is then adopted by the current Vidar and trained to be the next Vidar. Ariel is one of the most ruthless, most efficient killers this planet has ever produced. And she is your girlfriend, yet you knew none of this."

I felt ice in my veins. I wasn't mad at Ariel for not telling me about this. What explanation did she owe me? Also, how could I know if what Cindi was telling me was true? The answer was simple. I couldn't.

"Well, I guess I need to talk to Ariel about this then."

The color drained from Cindi's face. "Please don't tell her about me. I don't know what she would do."

I knew Ariel. At least it felt like I did.

"She wouldn't care, but I will keep your name out of it."

Cindi's face relaxed

"Thank you, Sammi."

— *Chapter 18* —

Fenrir's Bane

I MADE MY WAY back to the Hotel California. I took my folder out to begin homework. There was a small but sharp knock on my door. I opened it, and Ariel was standing there, looking like she had been through it. Dark circles under her eyes spoke of a sleepless night and a punishing day. Those green eyes bored into me like they always did.

"Hey, babe."

"Homework?" she asked, looking at the folders on my bed.

I nodded. "Yeah, but luckily, it is just reading."

She smiled fondly at the folders, as if remembering her time being grilled by the Norns. "Well, I could use a distraction. One of our best died in Pakistan earlier today."

I moved and sat at the small desk next to the bunk bed. "What happened?"

Ariel's shoulders slumped. "Bad luck mostly. He ran into a group of armed men on the way to take out their boss. They thought he was CIA, of course, or some other shadowy alphabet agency. They tortured him on live television. Based on the distance, we couldn't get to him in time, so in an act of mercy, Azrael, with my blessing, activated his chip. He slumped over, and that was it. He was a good man, Sammi. He was one of my father's oldest friends, so I wouldn't go anywhere near Valhol today."

This brought the previous conversation I had with Cindi back to the forefront of my mind. "Valhol? Othan is your father?"

"Yep, he is the old man. Quite the man if you knew his whole history. But it sounds like you are about to ask me another question so…pitter-patter."

I smiled, catching the *Letterkenny* reference.

"I had a conversation earlier with one of the students, and they told me how you became…well, you."

Ariel nodded, expressionless. "And what did this mysterious oracle tell you?"

I repeated what Cindi had said.

Ariel sighed and sat down on the bed.

"Sammi, what you heard is mostly true, but it is not the whole truth. The previous Vidar looks at all aspects of the potential candidate's morals and their driving force. They look at why more than they look at what. In the case of myself, my parents beat me and my little brother every day from about age two onward. My mom was a drug addict, and my father was a career criminal and an alcoholic."

She paused, looking away from me, as if steeling herself. Tears sprouted from the corner of her eyes. I reached out to tell her she didn't have to tell me, but she continued.

"One day my father beat my little brother so badly that he wouldn't get up. My mother laughed. She laughed at my little brother's tiny, broken body. I was quiet. I cradled his head in my arms, and he gurgled, trying to breath. A few minutes later, he died. I was six. He was four. When my parents finally passed out later in the night, my little brother's body was still laying in our living room. I went to the kitchen and got a chef knife. I snuck into their room and waited until I knew they wouldn't wake. I killed them both as they slept. And there I sat for thirty-six hours, covered in my parents' blood. Cradling my little brother's head. Hoping he would wake up. Until, finally, someone noticed my mom hadn't come into work, and the cops got sent to our little house on a wellness check. I guess the smell made them kick in the door. Or maybe the knowledge there were children in the house was what made them act."

The wells turned to streams as Ariel's breath caught. She fell forward into me. I held her for only a moment. She sat up.

"So…um…after that I was moved into a juvenile detention facility until I was nine. Then one day this guy named Othan showed up and asked me three questions. Did I regret what I did? Was I sad that my parents were dead? And how did I learn how to hurt them?

I answered his questions, and he said the words that would shape the remainder of my life."

She paused, smiled, and touched the dagger pendant around her neck.

"'Do you want to come with me and meet your new family?' He explained the rest to me on the car ride to the airport and then on the plane ride to Seattle. He told me that I had been officially adopted by him. The next day was the first day I called him Dad. He had my little brother's body exhumed and brought to Seattle for a real funeral and so I could visit him."

I listened to the whole tale, and my heart broke for her. With a still, small voice, I could only manage a question. "What was your brother's name?"

Ariel smiled and wiped some of the tears from her eyes.

"His name was Lance. He was very sweet. He used to steal little toys for me from his day care so I had something to play with. In return, I used to pocket food from school so he had something to eat at night."

I went and sat on the bed next to her. I put an arm around her and pulled her into my arms, hugging her tight, and the dreaded words came out in all their dark, baggage-laden glory.

"I love you, Ariel Vidar."

She cried quietly for a few moments. "I know."

When our bitter crying laughs subsided, she leaned up kissed me on the cheek.

"I love you too."

We stayed like that for a long time, just existing in each other's arms, not moving, not talking.

Ariel's head was on my chest. "I can hear your heartbeat."

I giggled. "My brain can't decide if that is really cute or really foreboding."

She looked up at me. "Why can't it be both?"

I kissed her, and we drifted off into a nap.

Chapter 19

Poor, Unfortunate Souls

THE VAN BOUNCED AND rattled as their team lead went over the plan again.

A thick Eastern European accent barked in the enclosed space.

"Alright, boys. The boss wants this quick, quiet, and dirty. Our element will take the east stairwell. We will clear floor by floor toward the other teams and then rinse, repeat. We will be clearing toward friendlies. Check your shots. Questions or concerns?"

The ten-man team in the back of the van was silent for a moment. The gloom of the Seattle night seemed to turn all the light coming through the front windshield into washed-out shades of oranges and yellow. The speed of the vehicle was making every bump feel like a pothole.

One of the operators spoke up, "Sir, what is our ex-fill plan?"

The large man standing in the middle of the bench seats said, "Code word Smoke will indicate that the mission is complete or that we need to pull out. We will then return to the vans and head to King County International. If for some reason you cannot make the ex-fill, you will E and E your way to the airfield. We are wheels up at zero six hundred hours local time. Anything else?"

No one spoke.

"Alright then. Comms on."

The men all checked their weapons one more time. The comms crackled to life on their ears, "All Overwatch elements set."

A few moments passed in silence.

"All Assault elements set," a colder, darker voice came over the comms.

"I have control. Execute."

As the vans converged from all directions on the building, the security guards near the elevator's banks slumped to the ground. Parts of their skull and brains decorated the stainless-steel doors behind them. Simultaneously all the lights in the building shut off.

The comm spoke again, "Jammers fully functional. No signals in or out. Lights are off. May God guide your hands."

The vans pulled into the parking structure at their four points of entry. The back doors of the vans opened, and all the operators made their way toward their particular door. The man on the left pulled on the door, but nothing happened. He tapped his helmet with his fist, and the second man placed a breaching charge on the door.

— Chapter 20 —

We Were Having a Moment, You Assholes

I woke with a start.

Ariel was already moving by the time I got my head off the pillow.

"Doc, initiate clean slate, dump all backups, and set charge timers to forty-five minutes. Evacuate all nonessentials to the Norn moot, barricade the door, and set Talon on Alamo. Then get Dagger recalled. Set the timer for CCR for nineteen minutes. Get my armor ready. Sammi and I are heading your way. Sammi, get your armor on and follow me."

I complied without a word. I slid my helmet on, and HITA said, "Comms up. Power is out. Outside comms are being jammed. TOC link is stable."

Ariel pulled her pistol from an unseen holster and press-checked it. I slid on my armor. Silently I thanked Edwin

"Okay, Sammi, we are going to have to run up the stairs and then to my office to form up with everyone."

I grabbed one of the pistols out of the case Ariel gave me and press-checked it. I picked up two spare magazines and slid them into the pistol mag pouches on my armor.

"Let's go."

Ariel moved like a woman possessed.

"They will be moving slow and careful. We need to outrun them and then counterattack."

A voice in my helmet stopped my question. "Sammi, can you hear me?"

"Yes."

Edwin's name popped up in my HUD, with a little mic icon next to it

"I saw on the security feed before it was cut. The corner stairwells have been breached. Approximately fifty guys with full kit. They are moving like professionals. I am under them, so I have no chance of getting out of here. How long until CCR?"

Remembering the letters Ariel had said, I said, "About eighteen minutes"

"Okay. Good luck, Sammi. If they make it in here, I will take as many with me as I can."

I was panicking and freaking out, but I shoved that deep down.

"I will not lose my composure in front of Ariel," I promised silently.

A dark, reptile part of my brain seemed to come alive. All that existed was the now, this moment; nothing else was real. The gray walls seemed to slide past as if without end.

"Doc, did you get that?" I called into the nothingness.

An ice-cold voice that I wouldn't have recognized as Doc's without the aid of the helmet icon said, "Good copy."

I repeated to Ariel what had been said as we ran the stairs two at a time.

"We are going to fuck these guys up. Fuck, they are blocking cell signals. We are going to have to rely on Azrael."

She pulled her sleeve up and yelled, "Prairie fire protocol entire northwest region, we are under attack."

We ran upstairs for what felt like an eternity, but the clock in my HUD said it was more like five minutes. Another timer showed up under the clock CCR thirteen minutes, twenty-seven seconds.

My breathing was coming in ragged huffing and puffing bursts by the time we made it to floor 56. We came through the door; two armed and armored assassins were waiting for us, and Ariel yelled.

"Blue, blue, blue."

The two operators stood from the corners they were holding and said, "Vidar, Doc is staged in your office and ready to move."

Ariel nodded and ran past them. I stayed right on her heels. I heard the door open again behind us. Ariel and I spun pistols raised toward the sound, but instead of armed interlopers Dr. Isley, Paton, and the trainees, Cindi at their head, came running in.

Ariel yelled, "Friendlies, let them through."

We then turned and continued running toward Ariel's office.

We heard behind us Dr. Isley scream. She had blood pouring down one of her arms and blood caking her cheek.

"They are killing everyone. Some of my people are down already, and they are moving up floor by floor."

Ariel said just loud enough for me to hear, "That's good. We need a little more time."

Disbelief washed over me, but I put it all away, forced from my mind the second I heard it.

"How long do we need?"

Ariel laughed. "I am not sure. Long enough for Bobby and Petra to take out the jammers and restore power. If we don't have power back by the time the CCR timer goes off, we aren't completely fucked, but this is going to be way fucking harder."

They crossed the threshold into Ariel's office. Doc and Phill were waiting for her, looking like space marines in their full-body armor, with their rifles, blades, and pistols at the ready.

"Doc, my armor."

He pointed at the desk. Ariel's armor and weapons were laid out ready.

She breathed a sigh of relief. "Well, at least we won't die like sheep."

She put on her armor and helmet quickly over her pajamas.

"Comm check."

Doc nodded. "Reading you, Lima Charlie."

"This was indeed the wrong house," Phill said, press-checking his rifle.

She nodded. "Okay, I need to coordinate with Talon before we do anything. Keeping the channel open." She press-checked her rifle.

"Talon Actual, this is Dagger Actual. How copy?"

A beat passed.

"This is Talon Actual. Good copy."

"I need half your team locking down the Norn moot. The rest I need as QRF, ready to respond to my commands."

I asked Doc quietly, "What does QRF mean?"

Doc sighed. "Quick reaction force."

"Will comply, Dagger Actual. Transferring Talon 2, 3, and 6 over to your command presently."

"I need a head count who made it to the moot and who didn't."

"We are missing several lab techs, and Dr. Isley just joined us. Edwin is locked in the armory. The only Norns here are Skuld and Verdandi. Urd was out this evening, and there were only ten members on sight all accounted for. Paton took a round before he could get off the matts. Several people from accounting HR and two Azrael are down hard. But reports are word of mouth. No confirmation without power."

Ariel nodded. "Okay. No reason for me to coordinate from here then."

My mind was swimming and overwhelmed by the motion and unfamiliar speech patterns of everyone around me. I was reminded of *Hitchhiker's Guide to the Galaxy*. "Don't panic."

Doc checked his med bag, slung it, and started toward the door.

"Where is the backup generator?" Ariel stated over an open comm channel.

"Bobby says that the power hasn't been cut. He says that it's a hack, some type of upload that made our part of the grid go into a diagnostic mode," Doc responded as he checked his grenades.

Ariel moved toward the door.

"Can he track it?" I asked over my helmet comm.

Phill and Doc followed on Ariel's heels toward the door.

"Yes, but he needs a little more time."

Ariel walked over to me and over a private comm said, "Go to the Norn moot with the others. Be Talon's backup."

I wanted to say, "No, I am coming with you. I go where you go," or some other macho, one-liner bullshit. But Ariel would just shoot me down and explain her reasoning. To which reasoning I would agree and comply, so I just said, "Got it," and made my way to the Norn moot.

— Chapter 20 —

They're in the Trees

Petra checked the time on her HUD as her Suburban hurtled toward Downtown Seattle. The familiar gray night was washed away by her ronin helmet's augmented-reality software, making the way bright as daylight. Bobby was typing on his laptop feverishly.

"Seven miles. Bobby, get me something."

Bobby bounced as they hit a bump in the road. He calmly stated, "I know. I will have it by the time we are in range."

Petra swung the Suburban through an intersection. Horns screamed as Petra blew past a red light and headed toward the building under siege.

Bobby finally exclaimed loudly over the comm channel.

"I've got them. It is one of the vehicles inside the parking garage. They disabled the backup generator as well. Which means our TOC is on battery backup. All nonessential systems are down. They are locked up there with an army between us and them."

Petra's driving became more frantic the closer they came to their target.

"Range?"

Bobby let a beat pass.

"Three miles. We can launch in four minutes."

"Oh, good, we have extra time," Petra said sarcastically.

Bobby's fingers flew over the keyboard, looking like a blur. Slowly all over the world the Arrangers were waking up and finding themselves at war.

Doc, Ariel, and Phill moved to the staircase and started working their way into position at the entrance of floor 55. At the door that led into the accounting department, they held position.

Ariel motioned at the door. "Prep concussion grenades."

Ariel pulled her grenade out, pulled the pin, and held the spoon tightly. Her HUD was alive with information. Updates poured into her chat feed on the right-hand side of her view. She heard Petra urging Bobby to get the drone in the air. The countdown timer on the helmet read one minute, thirty-four seconds.

Petra switched her HUD view to the handheld drone that Bobby had prepped for her and launched. She held the remote controller with the dexterity of a surgeon, as this was a task she had specifically trained for and executed hundreds of times before. The target was marked with a red triangle. The countdown timer in her helmet reached eighteen seconds as she flew into the floor-level parking area near the bank of elevators. The two Azrael guards that were normally on duty were dead on the floor. Pools of blood, black in the night vision of the drone. Six white vans were parked there, and the one with the red triangle was at the back. She dodged and weaved the drone into position under the marked van.

After it laid still on the ground beneath the fuel tank, she said, "Detonate."

The helmets onboard AI system complied.

Nine seconds left.

The team lead spoke into the comms aggressively.

"What do you mean our countermeasures are down? They have outside comms?"

As if in answer to his question, the lights came on and washed out his night vision for a moment. He flipped his NODs up, and what he heard he could not quite bring himself to believe.

From speakers seemingly all around, a female robotic voice exclaimed, "Welcome to the rice fields, motherfuckers."

Quietly at first and then so loudly he couldn't hear the response from his subordinates came…music. He recognized the music. "Fortunate Son" by Creedence Clearwater Revival blasted into the relatively tight quarters of the office bullpen. And the gun-for-hires' world turned white.

Ariel, Doc, and Phill's countdown timer hit zero They heard the start of the music. Ariel held up three fingers. She counted them down. Information flowed into their helmets' HUD now that power had been restored to the building. All friendlies were identified with the chips in their arms, registering them as such. All heat signatures in the building that did not coincide with an Azrael chip meant that their targets had now been painted for them.

Ariel's last finger descended. She popped the door open and tossed the concussion grenade through. Quickly closing it again, she waited for the telltale bang and then went through the door first.

For just a flash of a moment, her helmet's altered reality was washed out by blindingly white light. The sound of "Fortunate Son" blasted, but the helmet's built-in sound modulation cut it out of her feed entirely.

In less than a millisecond, her senses were full of nothing but the people she was about to kill. She went down the middle. Doc took the left, and Phill the right. In front of her were three men holding their ears and simultaneously trying desperately to free themselves of the night vision that they had been wearing before the emergency 120,000 Lumen floodlights filled the space with sunlike radiance—radiance that Ariel, Phill, and Doc's ronin helmets were filtering out.

Her suppressed rifle came to her eye and in turn shot each man center mass. They flinched as the seventy-seven grain Black Hills hollow points tore out their hearts.

Doc circled the large bullpen, expertly clearing through the dividers and past filing cabinets. A fire team of ten men stood in front of him, shielding their eyes, some covering their ears from the ripping music blasting into the space.

Doc smiled, knowing that this had somehow gone off without a hitch. Doc smiled for another reason; every single one of the men that had dared enter his lair were already dead. Their bodies had yet to be informed of this inescapable fact.

Doc lined up his rifle, his HUD doing most of the work, showing him where his bullet would land before the holographic sight even lined up on his first target. He squeezed the trigger, sending a round through his first target's nose.

The unsuppressed first shot made the men turn and fire wildly. One of the assaulters shot his ally in the midsection just below his plate carrier. Doc's smile widened as he took cover behind a pillar.

Amateurs, he thought to himself as he broke cover and emptied his magazine into them. Five were down. Doc transitioned to his pistol and shot the next three into the carpeted floor. Their blood sprayed in arcs and spurts onto their companions.

The two that were left seemed to be shocked into indecision. Doc paused and stepped back into cover, holstering his pistol and inserting a fresh magazine into his rifle. Knowing that he would probably be low on ammo in the next fight, he tightened the sling on his rifle and slung it over his back.

Using his right hand, he popped the bungie cord off his Cold Steel Norse Hawk. He was already closing with the first man as he drew the ancient weapon. He turned his wrist and imagined the hawk going through his opponent's head and sticking into the wall next to it. The blow landed on his foe's ear. He felt the crunch of cartilage and bone as the man dropped, wordless and soundless, to the ground.

Doc pulled his tomahawk free and planted it in the second man's knee. He deftly pulled it out, spun it in his hand, and smashed the man in the face with the blunt end. Inside the man's head, his brain bounced violently against, his skull sending him down, locked out into instant unconsciousness. Doc disarmed the man, removing a rifle, pistol, and several blades. Doc then zip-tied his arms behind his back and his legs together.

Phill sighted on his first target, who was feeling desperately along a wall for the staircase entrance that he had come in through. Phill looked at the distance on his HUD—eleven yards. He put two rounds through his target's brain stem and then moved on. Phill had the same thought as Doc, *The next gunfight would be worse. Save your ammo.* Another one of the intruders was stumbling around, trying to find his way in the blinding light and noise. Phill moved toward the man. He slung his rifle and reached behind his right shoulder, pulling out Snuggles.

Snuggles was the actual model name of Phill's favorite weapon. An eighteen-inch-long, three-pound, ten-ounce, modern-day Warhammer. It looked like a goth meat tenderizer with a spike on the back.

Phill indexed the familiar tool, and the RMJ tactical masterpiece slammed like a lightning bolt into the helmet of the confused man, dropping him to the floor. Phill spun the hammer in his hand so that the spike was facing outward. The man seemed to stir and reach upward. Phill drove the spike of the hammer through his downed opponent's face. He felt the spike drive into the man's skull, silencing him and stilling his movement forever. Phill whispered a prayer to the old gods and proceeded down the wall, finishing his grizzly work.

Ariel cleared through the middle of the office space toward the back set of stairs. "Clear."

Doc and Phill echoed her call, "Clear."

She called back, "All clear. Regroup on me."

The team lead fell into the stairwell, screaming, "Smoke, smoke, smoke!" over the comms.

Finally, someone responded, "First element is down hard. Second element is at half strength. It looks like these distraction tactics have happened on all floors cleared so far. Fourth element cannot get out of the parking-garage staircase. Some kind of blast door has sealed over the entrance."

The team lead screamed into his mic, "They are killing everyone. Get us the fuck out of here."

The man from Eastern Europe heard someone behind him speak in a metallic voice.

"Hey, asshole."

He turned toward the voice and saw a blur of motion at the top of the staircase. The light from the door above silhouetted a man that looked like an alien. The last thought that went through the man's mind was, *What is that thing? Why can't I see out of my right eye?* The man died a moment later, a tomahawk sticking out the right side of his head.

Doc slowly moved down the stairs to the landing where the man he just killed was laying. He reached down and pulled his tomahawk free from the man's head, saying, "You're no daisy."

He wiped the hawk off and put it back in its sheath over his right shoulder. "You're no daisy at all."

Ariel moved next to him and said, "Is there a chance, any chance whatsoever, that we can get through killing some motherfuckers and you won't hit us with spicy one-liners the whole time?"

Doc smiled and, in his best Joker impression, said, "Guns are too quick. They don't let you savor all the little emotions."

Ariel laughed. "You really should talk to someone."

"Well then, who would give the therapist therapy?"

Ariel sighed. "Fair enough. Let's get this done."

Phill looked at the guy on the ground. "Nice throw. I killed people with Snuggles."

The next floor was clear. Bodies were strewn among the bullpens. Ariel recognized a few of them, one she had seen earlier in a staff meeting. She stifled her tears for later and continued. Doc stopped at someone who grabbed his ankle as they passed. The experienced combat medic dropped, ran an IV, and put a chest seal on the wounded man.

"Hey, buddy. You are going to be okay. I'd give you a lollipop, but I'm fresh out."

The man started to make pained sounds. Doc checked him and confirmed he was stable.

"Need you to stay real quiet, buddy. Lots of bad guys around, okay? We will be back for you, I promise."

The man nodded, smiling in relief.

They approached the next floor. Ariel and Doc were on either side of the door. They raised their rifle barrels and lowered them in sync. They opened the door, and before they could get through, rifle fire began pinging off the doorframe.

Ariel slammed the door closed and called, "Talon 2, 3, and 6. Breach floor 52. Access stairs. Clear toward my pos."

"Copy, Dagger."

They waited and waited.

Two minutes had passed when the comm cracked to life.

"Dagger Actual, Talon 3 troops in contact."

Ariel nodded to Doc. "Good copy. Talon 3 clearing toward you. Watch the crossfire."

Ariel kicked the door open. Doc moved through, his rifle cracking as he walked. Ariel went down the middle and shot the man her HUD indicated was behind a filing cabinet. She shot him nine times through the metal furniture until his heat signature was slumped to the ground. Doc and Phill moved as one. Their HUDs displayed Talon's line of fire, and they moved laterally to simultaneously avoid friendly fire and to pin the remaining six highlighted targets. The preys that were predators had taken cover behind a bank of filing cabinets. Doc touched Phill's elbow as he swung out wide. Doc raised his rifle barrel, and Phill did the same. They burst from cover and closed with the gunman firing as they sprinted. All six were chewed up like bubblegum and spat out on the floor.

Ariel smiled silently to herself, seeing the carnage that her boys had wrought. It might not be pretty but, damn, was it effective. The two combined fire teams moved to the staircase to finish the job.

Doc looked over the railing and saw six guys all using a Halligan tool to try and peel the blast door open.

Doc said over the comm, "Based on Petra's report, these guys are it."

Ariel nodded.

Phill pulled out what looked like an oversized frag grenade, but it had multiple settings near the neck. He twisted the top to the position that said IMP. On the other side of the grenade, in white Sharpie, was written, "Fuck you in particular."

Phill pulled the pin, let the spoon go, and dropped the grenade over the banister. They didn't even hear it hit the floor.

A shockwave and a column of dust engulfed the staircase as the grenade detonated. All three of them looked over the banister a moment later to see six broken bodies lying at unnatural angles. Some moaned. Some screamed.

Doc slung his rifle by his side, "Yippie-ki-yay, motherfuckers!"

Ariel sighed and shook her head. "Fuck you, Doc."

— *Chapter 21* —

There Is Always a Bigger Fish

Ariel slung her rifle and keyed the open comm channel.

"Building clear. I repeat, building clear. All teams spread out and check for casualties. Someone get the self-destruct charges on the servers turned off. We don't need any more disasters this evening. We counted eighteen of ours down in total. Get them bagged and ready to move. Azrael is in route to assist. All non-operations personnel, there will be a meeting in the Norn moot in one hour. Attendance mandatory. Everyone, start gathering up your things. We are moving our circus to our secondary location until this problem is solved. Feather or heart."

A chorus answered her over the comm aggressively, "We balance the scales!"

Ariel spun on her heel and faced Doc. "How many did you take alive?"

Doc thought for a moment. "I got three. Not sure how many Connan and Snuggles over there got."

Phill smiled. "I took two alive. Snuggles doesn't take prisoners."

Doc laughed. Ariel's face was devoid of reaction.

"Go collect all the ones that can talk take them to my office now. Bring up a capsaicin kit and interrogation beds. Bring in Talon. I want it done in ten minutes."

They both nodded and started back into the building. Ariel keyed her comm to a private channel.

"Sammi?"

I responded quickly, "Hey, are you okay?"

"Yeah, babe, all good. We are going to have to relocate for the time being, but we will be back one day. I have some conversations to have with some of the survivors, and when I'm done with that, I am going to fuck your brains out."

A small pause—the kind that held terror for Ariel.

"Edwin is dead. Just heard from Talon a minute ago."

Ariel waited to gather her thoughts. "How did they get in?"

"The guy in charge of Talon says they blew their way in. But he also said Edwin took five of them with him."

Ariel could tell Doc just got the news when his helmet went offline a moment later. No doubt something had just been smashed with said helmet. Ariel knew what to do next.

"I'll call you later, babe. For now, I have a little work to do."

Ariel looked at the bound and gagged men tied naked to the interrogation tables. Ariel said nothing for several seconds.

The men looked around the office in confusion. They were probably confused as to why they weren't in police custody. Ariel pulled her Karambit from its sheath on the small of her back. She deftly cut the gags off each of the men.

Slowly Ariel walked over to a rolling silver table, where she picked up a syringe full of clear liquid. She pushed out a few drops and walked to the first table. She held open the man's eyelid and let one drop go onto the man's exposed eyeball. The reaction from the strapped-down man was instant. He screamed and squirmed and struggled. Ariel's face was hard, cold, and empty. She delivered one drop into the eyes of each of the men.

"Tell us what you want," one screamed.

"Come on, I have kids!"

Ariel ignored them. With them, her humanity. Her recently donned high heels clicked against the polished floor. Their echoes like tolling bells marked passing moments of agony and screaming.

The screams finally died down.

"Hello, and welcome to Arrangements by Ariel. I, as some of you may know from your pre-mission briefing, am Ariel. What I just dropped into your eye is 98 percent capsaicin and 2 percent vodka.

Now, who wants to sell out their boss and join our team? I need at least two new security guards, thanks to you witless fucks."

The men were silent. Ariel knew this part of the process well. It was a game. First one to talk loses.

Finally, one of the men spoke up. His Russian accent was near indecipherable, yet his words were simple.

"Fuck you, you stupid suka."

Ariel smiled at the naked man, silently thanking him for advancing the game forward.

"So let me explain the rules of this little back-and-forth that we all find ourself in tonight. One of you fine, young men are going to tell me who hired you. You will tell me all the information that this person gave you. You will then point my colleagues to every known contact safe house and talent provider that you went through to arrive in this man's service. The one of you that does this will get a new job and will live. The ones of you who don't… Well, I will have the best interrogator in the world come in here and use that stuff on you for days. Until, eventually, your hearts give out and you die. They will isolate the truth out of you, and you will have no choice. Let's do this the easy way and cut out the middleman. She costs three thousand an hour, so I want to avoid paying her if I can. Give me what I need, and we can all put tonight behind us."

They all started talking at once.

"Calm down, boys, and save it."

They were silent again. At a motion, four of her intelligence analysts and a uniformed member of Talon stepped into the room

"You will tell these nice people everything that you know, and then I will decide what to do with you based on the results. Everyone going to behave?"

They all nodded furiously.

Ariel smiled. "Good boys."

— *Chapter 22* —

Ariel the Human

Ariel put the file down on her desk. She looked at each of her teammates in turn. A mixture of pride, trust, and love welled up in her.

"We will mourn for Edwin when the time comes." She glanced at each of them before she continued. "But for now, we have a name. Better than that, boys and girls, we have an enemy."

Ariel dumped the file on the table and gave them a minute to read the bullet points. Lots of murmuring and headshakes went around the table.

"Boss, how are we going to do this? This guy is off-limits."

Ariel shook her head. "Nothing and no one is off-limits, even us."

They nodded in unison.

Ariel continued, "Now, you guys start putting screws in this guy. I want everything. I want to understand the whole picture yesterday. We have never been tested like this. We will not forgive them because they knew not what they did."

All heads around her nodded. She felt tired. Mentally exhausted from the day's events, spending a little time with Sammi felt right before they left. She went to her room on the fifty-fourth floor and showered the grime of battle off.

* * * * *

I spent most of the assault heroically guarding people that were scarier than me. I had gone to the barracks after the happy news came from Ariel earlier.

Big high fives and backslapping hugs had been the response from everyone. They all treated me as if I personally saved each one of them.

I was packing my meager belongings away when I noticed something in my backpack that wasn't there before. B-Don's cigarette case and his Zippo lighter. A tear started forming at the corner of my eye, sparking a memory of B-Don.

I pointed accusingly at the tear and said, "Get back in there!"

I missed my friend. This thought reminded me of Zarov. My hate felt warm in my stomach. The sheer number of impossible things over the last few weeks made me dizzy. My inner monologue betrayed my insecurity.

"Imposter syndrome? More like 'not good enough to be in the same zip code as Ariel' syndrome."

My girlfriend, who was probably on her way down here, had just sealed in and executed a large group of men that were sent here to kill us all. And she did so with what felt like no remorse. I had started to wonder without too much prompting by any outside force, were we really the good guys? No one seemed to ever question that, which worried me greatly.

Then I remembered something Ariel said, "Stop worrying if you are the good guy."

At the end of the day, there was no real way for me to tell for sure.

A gentle knock rapped against my door. The interruption, while expected, jolted me out of my reverie. All the thoughts I just had were banished in the instant Ariel arrived.

I cracked the door open. Ariel stood there in a Hello Kitty nightgown with a six-pack of beer.

"You know anyone that could help me drink these?"

I smiled. "I might know a guy."

She walked in, somehow making the plain, corny evening gown sexy. She pulled two beers from their cardboard prison and deftly popped them open. She handed me one.

"Nihil vivit aut frustra moritur."

We clinked out bottles together.

"What does that mean exactly?"

An eyebrow raised, she tipped her beer skyward, then she gave me a look as if to say, "Why do you still have clothes on?" She sat her beer down and indulged me.

"When a weak member of a colony of ants dies, it does not die in vain. Its death reduces the resource load on the colony, and if the ant died before reproducing, it removes its DNA from the species pool. Thus, increasing their strength by removing a weakness. Nothing, and I mean nothing, on this planet by the very definition of nature lives or dies in vain. Whales that die eventually float to the bottom of the ocean and give life to thousands of species that live in the crushing darkness. With this definition of usefulness, no individual creature in this world can live or die in vain."

Ariel came within grabbing distance as I sat in the small office chair. She reached out her bottle. We clinked bottles again. I drained the rest of my beer; she did the same.

Ariel said mournfully, "I'm tired, Sammi. I get why Othan retired at fifty. I understand now why my father is the way he is. It's too much. All of it is just too much for one mind to oversee."

I reached out and pulled her into a tight embrace, letting her get out the baggage that needed venting.

"I don't know what I am supposed to do next. My father, grandfather, and great-grandfather never had to deal with anything like this. They just ran the moot, hit their targets, and moved on. They never had this level of scrutiny where we must come up with more and more elaborate plans to keep ourselves hidden. Have any idea what we are telling the cops?"

I shook my head.

"We are telling them that the blackout and subsequent noise complaints that went out a little while ago was an impromptu corporate party. That some employees got ahold of some fireworks, and it got a little out of hand, but everything is fine. If they would have taken the time to search our grounds for more than a cursory stop at the front desk, we would have been screwed. Well, not completely screwed. I guess we can always relocate—new names, passports, all that good stuff—but it is never as good as the real thing. Fortunately, the mayor and the chief of police are friends of mine. And this was taken care of with a quick phone call."

I was silent and waited to see if there was more she needed to get out. When a minute had passed, I said, "Ariel, you have one of the hardest jobs in the world. I have no idea what you are supposed to do. Maybe what you need to do is get outside of your problem to understand it better. Get back to your roots, touch some grass, something like that."

Ariel smiled a big, cheesy grin. "I think you may have just solved my problem."

I leaned in and kissed her cheek. She bit my lip in response. I almost threw her on the bed then and there, but something told me she wanted to talk more.

"Did I? Well, call me Dr. Phil."

She giggled, her face inches from mine "Okay, Dr. Phil, but when I'm screaming your name in a bit, it might throw the mood off."

How did she always know what to say to make me laugh?

"You say throw the mood off. I say we just discovered a kink I didn't know I had."

She snorted. I kissed her playfully, she pulled away.

"I know who came after us tonight, and getting to him is going to be, at best, fucking hard."

"What is his name?"

"That's classified."

I shook my arm at her. "Death chip. I have a large stake in keeping my mouth shut."

She laughed and nodded. "Well, in that case. His name is Aldrich Alecto. He is a hyper-empowered individual from Croatia. His fingers are in everything oil, cobalt, liquid natural gas, lithium, shipping, and most importantly, for our purposes, his day-to-day job is political operative. He has connections to all our most important allies. The very few people who make sure our bills are paid and grant us access to the black budgets are his allies as well. So, basically, at the end of the day, we work for the same people. With that in mind, he is untouchable. And guess who revealed a connection between Alecto and Edward Gallo?"

I shook my head. "Zarov."

Ariel nodded. "Some of the men hired to liquidate us work directly for Mr. Alecto. Which means that Zarov has found a new boss. Or maybe he just got promoted. A boss with massive connections across the globe. With this patronage, he could do anything. Zarov just became much harder to kill."

I sighed. "Well, one upside is, that gives me more time to finish my training."

"True, and you are already on an abbreviated timeline."

I thought for a minute. "Where are we heading next?"

She jumped up. "Well, what do all good cowboys do after they take a licking? We are heading to Mexico."

I stared bug-eyed at her. "Wait, really?"

"A lot, and I mean a lot, of our flowers come from southern Mexico and Ecuador. So we already have a headquarters there. We will give some bullshit line to the legitimate part of our business about remodeling our headquarters and wanting our employees to be closer to the land. Something like that, then we will head down. Phill will handle the details and optics."

I shook my head "Phill? Like our Phill? The Warhammer-wielding, skull-splinting, joke-cracking Phill?"

She nodded and scrunched up her face. "Yeah, he is our communications director. He always handles any work we do with the public."

I shook my head in disbelief. "Really?"

She nodded. "He has a master's degree in public relations and cooperate communications."

"Holy shit," I said, genuinely surprised. "If they only knew."

"It has been a running joke since he came onboard about five years back. The guy with a Warhammer named Snuggles is out there, being the face of the company." Ariel jumped off me and sat down on the bed. "You know, sweetie, we probably aren't going to see each other for a while after the move happens tomorrow."

I tilted my head. "Tired of me already?"

She shook her head. "No, you ship out to Tampa, Florida, with Doc and the other students for a month of tactical training tomorrow morning. You are going to come back useful."

"I would like that change of pace because right now I am a potato person that you like banging out with."

Her mood shifted to serious. "Do you want to know why I like you?"

I felt a trap in the question, but I bit anyway. "Sure."

"The reason is simple. To you, I am not Ariel the Assassin or Ariel the Billionaire, nor am I Ariel the Bachelorette that you conquered. I am just simply Ariel the Human. Because I can see that truth in your eyes, I feel like a person, not an object that could be useful to you."

I thought about her brother that was killed in front of her. I thought about the weight of that moment for one so young. I thought about her killing her parents. I thought about the words that Othan etched into my brain as if with an iron chisel: "You will never find peace that lasts."

And yet, in this moment, peace there was. Maybe not a lasting one but my soul felt at peace. I felt certain and secure in the knowledge that the person in front of me was raw, honest, dependable, and caring. She was equal parts demon and angel. She was a taker of lives and a giver of lives. I felt understanding for the paradox that was Ariel Vidar. No one could have said it better. She was human. All her flaws were there laid out in front of me, and I didn't care. I accepted her in her entirety. I thought of B-Don and how much he would have liked her. This made a tear well in the corner of my eye. She leaned up and wiped it with a thumb.

"Why are you crying?"

I smiled; no words came out. Words could not give meaning to this mote of time. I kissed her gently, but with intent. She wrapped her hands around the back of my head and pulled me onto her.

She did not fuck my brains out. There was no desperation. No frantic need. Only two humans who loved each other, finding a reason to continue living in this world, a world that hid meaning like a priceless treasure peeled open, like a bomb blowing open a dam. We stayed in each other's arms for what felt like an eternity. Ariel's green, luminescent eyes bored into mine, and our rhythm found a steady pace. She kissed my neck as my orgasm ripped through me like a tidal wave breaking down any remaining emotional barriers. After her climax subsided, the dreaded words came unbidden.

"I love you."

She pecked my nose with a small kiss. "I love you too."

Many hours passed as we both came in and out of sleep. Ariel's phone went off, and she woke with a start. I sat up, and she punched me square in the nose. I saw stars as I fell out of the bed. My eyes welled up, and blood flowed like a waterfall.

Ariel vaulted out of the bed. "I am so fucking sorry… Fucking god, I didn't mean to."

She was freaking out and fussing over me. If blood wasn't gushing out of my nose, it would have been endearing.

"Quartermaster," she yelled.

A microsecond later Denny's old-man voice came over an overhead speaker. "Yes, Vidar."

"Get in here with an ice pack and some gauze in a hurry."

"Yes, Vidar."

She held a washcloth under my nose, catching the blood. "I am so sorry, Sammi."

I was still coming out of the daze her punch put me into. "It's fine, babe. I didn't mean to startle you."

Ariel shook her head. "The phone went off, and I was in a deep sleep. I am so fucking sorry. I never want to hurt you. Please don't hate me."

I laughed. "Hate you? After that nice reminder on the importance of head movement?"

She laughed sadly. A moment later, Denny came in the room and immediately shielded his eyes at the sight of the two naked people on the ground.

"Um, Vidar, I have the ice pack and gauze."

She nodded. "Thank you, Denny. Leave them on the coffee table, please."

Denny laid the ice pack and gauze on the table.

"Hey, Denny."

"Hello, young sir. Having a rough evening?"

I nodded. "Yeah, I zigged when I should have zagged."

"Well, better luck next time. Have a good evening. No more rough stuff."

I laughed. "We promise."

Denny, his eyes covered, left the room quickly. We both started laughing uncontrollably.

"Well, Denny has seen us naked now. Does that make us friends?"

I nodded. "Yeah, I think that's the rule. Once someone has seen you naked that you must talk to again, that puts them squarely in the friend category."

The laughter quitted, and a seriousness returned to Ariels countenance. "Again, I am so sorry about hitting you. It was not my intention."

I smiled while holding the ice to my nose. "No problem. At least I will have a story to tell Doc that will probably have some domestic-violence jokes in it."

She smiled wryly. "Well, if you want, you can talk to HR director about some pain and suffering pay."

I laughed. "How scary is the HR director?"

Ariel smiled. "She is former Mossad, Kidon unit. She has killed more people than cholera and has a deep interest in psychedelic interrogation techniques."

I shook my head. "I…um…think I'm good."

Ariel laughed. I thought about asking Ariel if she was okay, but thought better of it. She would tell me what was going on when she was ready to.

"Want to go check on Doc?"

Ariel thought about it and spoke. "Yeah, let's do that. Grab the last two beers, and we will head up. He is probably in his office."

A few minutes later, once clothes were dawned and the ice pack placed on the nose, we headed up to floor 56.

People were milling around, some carrying boxes full of books. Others were carrying animal mounts out of Ariel's office. Others were scraping labels off office doors. Other people were talking quietly or crying while others consoled them.

Ariel struck quite the image, moving down the hallway of professionals all doing their job while she was wearing a Hello Kitty nightgown with a beer in her hand. They all nodded to her as she walked past. We came to the end of the hallway, where we heard, "Fuck that, fuck that! We are going to kill everyone. I am going to go to his house in the middle sh…of the night, and then I am going to fuck him and then his dad."

"No, you're not. You are going to wait for the moot and Ariel to give you permission, and then we will say hello."

We made it to the office of the senior florist of Arrangements by Ariel. Doc was obviously very drunk. And Phill was going shot for shot with him.

"What are you two knuckle draggers doing?"

They both looked up. Doc had a bottle of Jameson in his hands that was half empty.

"ShVidar, what a pleasant surprise. Come in. Can I interest you in some whiskey? Holy shit, what happened to your face, Sammi?"

I smiled, ice pack pressed against my throbbing nose. "Oh, this? I overcooked the meat loaf again, and in my rush to get it out of the oven, I fell down some stairs."

Doc was taking another slug of whiskey, which he promptly sprayed all over Phill in response to my answer.

A few minutes later, the rest of Direct-Action Team Dagger arrived in the office, filling up the remainder of the space. Petra, Bobby, Eli, and Rook all filed into the room.

Bobby spoke first. "All tasks set have been completed as requested, Vidar."

Ariel took a long swig from the whiskey bottle, pausing for a moment. "You have all done well. Now let's get hammered."

They all laughed and began passing the rest of Doc's Jameson around the group. Petra and Rook abstained and left several minutes later.

Bobby swigged deep from the bottle and spoke, "Hey."

All eyes turned to him.

"Anyone else think they're fuckin'?"

The group laughed. Doc pulled an electronic weed pen from his desk, slurring his words. "Shwell, if they are, I say, good for them."

Bobby and Phill echoed him. "That's what I said. I said, good for them."

Doc took a big hit off his pen and said, "To be fair."

All members present including Ariel sang, "To be *fair*."

Doc did a little gesture with his hand, cutting them all off in unison.

Bobby picked up the string. "To be fair, if you think about it, people in the org are the only people we really can fuck."

Doc nodded in his drunken haze. "Welsh, tits not so bad when they don't know your name, address, or where you work. The problems start when"—he made a throwing-up gesture—"feelings start getting involved."

Ariel nodded. "That is where the problem lies, Rufio."

Doc laughed. "Lookie, lookie, I've got a hooky." Doc pulled a knife from somewhere and stabbed it through the file labeled Aldrich Alecto.

Ariel sighed even though she understood; this was not her favorite side of the mohawk-laden operator.

I raised my beer, starting to feel a little drunk myself. "Edwin."

All drinking utensils in the room raised in salute.

"The best armorer that ever lived." I didn't even know up to that point how true that statement was.

"May he await our arrival in Valhalla." Phill raised his beer higher.

"Till Vanhalen, brother," Doc slurred.

They all drank, and silence ruled the room for a bit.

Ariel finally broke the silence. "Alright, Doc, get to bed. You have an early flight. The rest of you, follow up with all action items before you hit the sack."

They all nodded.

On her way out, she leaned to Phill's ear. "Make sure he goes to bed and doesn't go on an adventure."

Chapter 23

Doc's Adventure

Doc threw a paper clip at Phill, who was dozing off. Everyone had left what felt like to Doc quite a long time ago.

Phill nodded awake. "What the fuck?"

Doc threw another paper clip at his friend seated in the chair.

"Okay, what the actual fuck?" Phill barked.

Doc smiled. "Hey, wanna go on an adventure? I have a great idea."

"No, you heard the Vidar. No adventures."

"Boo. No, I wanna go out. Look, it's still early. One a.m. we have plenty of time for what I have in mind."

Phill pulled his arm away from Doc, who had now come around the corner of his desk.

"Look at me, Phill. I just want to go out for one drink, maybe see a few familiar faces, and then back here. One beer adventure, Phill. Come on. Let's go."

Phill did not move. "You heard her. No going outside. No telling fortunes, no stealing gas out of people's cars, no horse racing, and most fucking certainly, no fighting. No fucking fighting!"

Doc smiled. "Of course, Mr. Shelby, I won't go outside. I will be in a car for half the adventure. The other half will be in a bar. Not outside, and as for the rest, I don't know how to bet on horses, but I kinda wanna learn. I only told that one lady her fortune that one time so she would play with my giant pee-pee. Just kidding. It's tiny, but wide like a tuna can. And me fight? When have you ever known me to pick a fight?"

Phill was still laughing at the tuna-can joke when the last sentence finally hit him.

"Oh, yeah, never you. Only like 90 percent of the times we have gone out."

Doc drooled out the second half of that shot he just took. "Pshhh, it was only like half of them tops."

Phill shook his head. "You know what, fuck it. Let's go."

Ten minutes and one blessedly automated car ride later, Doc and Phill arrived at Slammers, their favorite dive bar in Seattle. Doc fell asleep twice on their car ride, but resurrected himself when KITT said, "You know, Ariel will find out that you guys 'borrowed' me, right?"

"Well, she won't if you are nice and, ya know, just don't tell her," Phill begged.

"Listen, you fucking silly meat bag, Ariel Vidar will find out, eventually. But I won't volunteer the information."

"Thanks," said Phill, resigning himself to his fate.

Phill and Doc walked into Slammers. The bartender immediately had two beers and two shots of chilled Zyr vodka poured for them.

They nodded their thanks, and Doc said, "Look ofver there."

Phill followed his friend's eyeline and saw three local assholes that Doc and Phill had helped remove from Slammers a few months back.

Phill sighed. "Do we have to?"

Doc smiled stood and walked over to the three men. Doc felt more sober every step he took toward the three.

"Hello again, you silly fucks. It looks like you don't know how to read a room, so allow me to assist. The three of you have come back to this fine establishment after me and my friend over their told you to leave and not to come back."

The three men stood. One was larger than Doc, around six feet seven inches.

"What the fuck are you going to do about it?"

Doc smiled and slammed the cold shot of vodka.

"Well, that's the rub. We can't fight in here. This is sacred ground. But outside? That ground is not sacred at all. Wanna play?"

The large one started toward Doc, and Doc backpedaled toward the front door. Phill sighed heavily. Edwin's death had hit Doc hard, and this was part of him coping. What these large, belligerent men did not know was, they were about to be part of Doc's healing process. Phill slammed his shot and then walked quickly out the front door. Doc and his new old friends followed behind.

Phill turned in the parking lot to face the front door. Doc was removing his breakables and then walked to the car. Phill and Doc in turn disarmed themselves, placing their pistols and blades back in the Phantom before locking the car with the weapons inside it.

The largest of the three goons opened his soon-to-be closed mouth. "You pussies going to do something or just stand there?"

Doc rolled his shoulders, smiling, and walked forward. Phill, on his left, followed close behind.

"I have a feeling you were not burdened with an overabundance of schooling," Doc intoned.

The large man ran at Doc, trying to tackle him. Doc sprawled, and the man's head hit the pavement hard. Doc's hands were on the back of the man's head. He pounded the man's head twice into the ground before a blow to the side of Doc's head sent him spinning to the asphalt. He rolled up to his feet and squared off with the man on the right. The man on the left swung at Phill, but he was off-balance. Phill parried the clumsy blow and slid his hand down the length of the man's arm, grabbing the back of his head. Phill stepped forward and slammed the crown of his head onto the man's nose. The man fell with a spray of blood. The last man standing took a couple of exploratory jabs at Doc, who slipped the first; and when the second came, he slipped low and left, coming up out of the evasive maneuver with a massive blow to the man's lower ribs. The man culched his side and fell over in a heap.

Phill walked over to Doc, who was wibbly-wobbling and threatening to fall over. Phill put one of his arms over Doc's shoulder.

"That was a textbook liver punch, buddy."

Doc smiled drunkenly. "Neato Mosquito."

"Okay, let's get you home. That's enough fun for the night. Shit, I need to close our tab."

"Leave now? I have not yet begun to defile my s-shelf. Tab's closed though. Left 'em a couple hundreds of dollars before I walked over to our, um…friends."

He motioned at the men on the ground, who looked miserable. Doc threw a hundred-dollar bill on each man, saying, "Buy your self's somethin' nice."

"Okay, let's go, buddy." Phill got him back in the car, where Doc promptly fell asleep.

— *Chapter 25* —

OODA

Our flight to Tampa happened without ceremony. When the plane landed, and the doors opened. The hot, sticky, humid grossness of Florida blasted me in the face. I headed to baggage claim, where Doc had beaten me.

"Hey, buddy, how was the flight?"

"Not bad. I was sandwiched between a refrigerator person and a screaming baby. How was yours?"

"I see our Vidar is making careful efforts to not show favoritism. I had a nice, hot towel after the flight, and during I had a three-course meal."

I shook my head vigorously, "You…fucking flew first class?"

Doc's smile lit up the baggage area.

"Of course. It wouldn't do for the senior florist to ride in coach with the peasants now, would it?"

The drive to the secret training facility took only an hour. Once there, the man at the gate scanned Doc's arm and took a retinal scan. He did the same to me.

Doc smiled as we entered the massive facility. There were CONEX containers that had been set up as barracks and a massive, rectangular building that simply said "Fuel" on it. I surmised quickly that this was the eating and general assembly area. As the walk continued, Doc finally pointed to a mean-looking man in a Grunt Style T-shirt, where around forty recruits were standing in a semicircle.

Doc nudged me and spoke, "That's you. Big guy has you from here."

I extended my hand to Doc's, saying, "Thanks for everything, man. Next time I see you, you are an instructor, yeah?"

Doc nodded. "You are most welcome, sweet man. I'll see you soon."

Doc headed toward the Fuel building.

I walked up to the large man wearing a backward Oakley's cap and a Grunt Style T-shirt that said, "Fuck your feelings," on it.

He looks like he is fun at parties, I thought to myself.

The instructor looked at his tablet and counted again.

"Howard?" He asked.

Because I love movies, I knew the correct answer was, "Yes, sir!"

He smiled. "Well, now, isn't that sweet. I am not a fucking sir, son. I am the hand of the almighty here to provide you know-nothings with an acceptable level of lethality and survivability. You may call me Instructor Clint. Dude, bro, or brother will be met with an immediate and hilariously lopsided ass-beating. Do you understand?"

I nodded and said, "Yes, Instructor Clint."

"Fantastic. Your ears are functional. Get in line."

I complied.

Instructor Clint stepped to the head of the group.

I was standing next to Cindi, who elbowed me and spoke, "Mommy's favorite couldn't be on time, huh?"

"Fuck you, Cindi" I said, smiling.

She smiled back. Instructor Clint ignored our quiet back-and-forth.

"Good morning, trainees. I am Instructor Clint. Over the next month, I will personally—with the assistance of other team members—teach each and every one of you useless fuck sticks how to stop the human heart and keep yours beating. I do not care what unit you have come from or if you are a civilian off the street." He eyed me. "Everything you have been taught by your previous units was probably four to ten years out of date, so do everyone here and yourself the favor of assuming you know nothing."

No one made a sound as he paused.

"You are here to carry on a tradition that has kept humanity out of the void successfully. The men, women, and those not otherwise classified that have trained in this facility have gone on to do things you have never heard of that allow us to have this conversation now. When I give you a command, you will respond with the words, 'Feather or heart,' to indicate your understanding. Your classmates will respond, 'We balance the scales,' to indicate they also heard the command and will assist you when needed.

"This call and response go back to the first meeting Gregory Vidar had with Wild Bill Donovan at the inception of our organization. When discussing the ethos this organization should hold, Gregory said to Bill, 'We will be a blade in the darkness that will quell or exonerate all that fall on our edge. Like the scales of Anubis, we shall measure them and judge the purity or corruption of each action taken by them and by those judgements humanity will survive, feather or heart.' To which Bill responded, 'We balance the scales.' Some of you that go on to be Azrael will notice that there was no exemption given to members. Our hearts also reside on the scale. Your actions here will be judged and measured until they arrive at my standard. Or you will not be on the direct-action or security side of the house. Is that understood?"

Having listened earlier, the trainees responded correctly. Thank God.

"Yes, Instructor Clint."

"So you all understand, this is a no-fail mission that I have been tasked with. You will be held to the same standard I am held to. Sammi, since you are the least-experienced person here, you will act as team leader."

The color drained from my face, but his instructions prompted my tongue. "Feather or heart."

The whole class behind me finished the refrain, "We balance the scales."

The first task we were commanded to undertake was to sit and load one thousand magazines. Five hundred with 5.56 mm and the other five hundred with 7.62x39. and then put them into ammo cans. I watched as my team meticulously loaded, and I did the same. After two hours, the task was done. Instructor Clint walked down the lines of tables that the ammo cans sat on. He opened one and pulled out a magazine holding 7.62 that was in the 5.56mm can. He pointed at me and waved me over. I walked briskly to meet him, my expression blank.

"Howard. What the fuck is this?"

I saw what was in his hand, and my heart sank. "A mistake, Instructor Clint."

"A mistake… Do you think we have held chaos at bay by allowing for mistakes, son? How would you make sure that this type of mistake did not happen again?"

"I am sorry, Instructor Clint. I would make sure to double-check the ammo cans for the correct magazines next time."

Clint smiled an evil, ugly smile. "Well, isn't that constructive. I am not sure why you apologized to me. I am not who you should apologize to."

I looked around as if to say, "Who then?"

Clint pointed at a palm tree sprouting from a flowerbed in front of the Fuel building.

"You will go apologize to the trees for wasting the oxygen they worked so hard to make for you. You want to apologize. Don't come back until the tree believes your apology."

Laughter was concealed by my classmates, but resigned to my fate, I nodded and ran toward the palm tree. I apologized to the tree for three hours until Clint told me to get back to work.

The next month went by in a blur at the training center. I learned how to shoot a pistol, a rifle, and how to use foreign weapon platforms. The running… Jesus Christ, the running. I did not know before these months of training how much I hated running. I learned about poisons and how to spot surveillance efforts. I learned how to be dropped off in a city with twenty dollars in my pocket and get everything I needed to end a human life. I learned how to rappel, jump out of an airplane, and how to scuba dive. I learned small-unit tactics, large-unit tactics, solo tactics, hand-to-hand combat, and knife-fighting. I learned how to operate a bolt gun and how to operate a shotgun. By far the coolest part of the training was how to operate a vehicle in emergency situations. Most importantly, I came to rely on my team. From big things like repairing an engine in a suburban to little things like when and how to take a knee in a gunfight so that if you get hit, you don't fall into the line of fire. Every night before bed, I saw images of B-Don and Zarov play through my mind's eye. I could see the hurt and the desperation on B-Don's features. I tried to banish the images and see him how he was—a cigarette in one hand and a beer in the other. But my desired image never came. Just the horror. I missed Ariel. She made all the horror either go away or made its presence a worthy trade.

The muscle-bound Instructor Clint yelled in my ear as the targets danced on the range. "OODA, motherfucker do you speak it? Orient, observe, decide, act! You are spending all your time on the Os. Get the D in that A before I fuck your mother in the middle of Times Square wearing a Superman costume!"

I smiled and fired, hitting all four moving targets center mass, breaking each shot in cadence.

"My mother is dead, Instructor Clint."

The gorilla in a Grunt Style T-shirt yelled with glee, "Good! I have a shovel!"

Dr. Isley's modifications had done their job. I was faster stronger and far more agile. I could almost feel myself over the months turn from a simple person into something else. My brain became a blade. On top of all the cool things, I learned basic combat medicine, and the whole time I was required to read up on human anatomy. Doc had called the training, "How to make holes and plug holes."

Doc spoke loudly to the class. He cranked down on a tourniquet, showing us the correct way. Cindi squealed as it closed.

"If it hurts, it is probably on. But check for a pulse near the ankle." He showed us the correct spot just behind the ball joint in the ankle. "If you can't feel a pulse, it's closed. You will then check for secondary wounds. Many times, the wounds you see will not be the wound that kills your patient."

I was feeling confident. Ariel and I talked at least once every couple of days. We watched *Battlestar Galactica* over our laptop screens together when time permitted. When the last day of training came, it was a mock-up of a real tactical environment on a simulated city street. The goal was to find your target while positioning yourself well in the pretend crowd of people and to execute them without anyone noticing. When all was said and done, I had gone from bartender to competent assassin in less than three months.

Doc and Instructor Clint stood at the front of the class in the Fuel building.

Instructor Clint spoke loudly, "Congratulations, you have survived your training. What happens next is up to the personnel department, but I can promise you, wherever you go on this big blue marble, you will always have friends that you made in this room. Believe in them, and they will believe in you. Because at the end of the day, we are all we have. We stand alone together. Feather or heart."

The room answered the mantra as we had all throughout training, "We balance the scales."

Doc stepped away from the lectern and sauntered over to me.

"Hey, buddy."

I smiled. "That was a nice speech."

Doc shrugged. "Yeah, he practices it in the mirror wearing a banana hammock."

"Hot."

"Are you heading to Mexico?"

I shook my head. "No idea. I guess I will just wait for the personnel department."

Doc smiled a knowing smile. "Sure, you will."

About an hour later, Ariel called me. "Hey, babe."

"That's killer babe to you now. I am basically a ninja."

"You do look good in pajamas."

"Where are you planning on posting me?"

A pause. "I am not sure yet. The moot voted on Alecto weeks ago, and we are currently planning an op to get Zarov and him at the same time. We are pretty sure they are holed up near our Montenegro office, so we will probably meet there in a few days."

"Understood. Just let me know. It will be nice to see Zarov in the flesh. I see him in my dreams every night."

Ariel waited a beat. "Well, soon you will be able to reach out and touch him."

My thoughts went to a metal chair, a gag, blood, my friend dying on the floor next to me. Me powerless to do anything to help. Zarov laughing. It all went together in my mind and sharpened itself into a white-hot spike of hate.

"I am going to kill him."

Ariel laughed. "No more pencils, no more books, no more teachers' dirty looks."

I laughed. "I am going to do terrible things to you when I see you, things that would make a dominatrix blush."

Ariel laughed, low and sultry. "Promises, promises."

"I love you, babe. Call me when it's time to leave."

"I will. Probably best to go ahead and start packing. Love you too."

The text from Ariel came an hour later: *Driver on their way to take you to the airport. He will have your ticket. You better sleep on the plane because when you get here, there will be no sleeping xoxoxo.*

— *Chapter 26* —

Alecto

ALDRICH LOOKED OUT OF the third-story window of his nineteen-thousand-square-foot home in Budva's Old Town district. The compound faced an old church, and it reminded him of his upbringing. Warm, calm, loving memories of church and his grandmother taking him to mass flowed for a moment and took him from his weighty life.

He liked the sounds of the old city wafting up on the nighttime breeze. He sipped from a glass of Louis XXIII cognac that was re-aged and rebottled. Alecto rolled the tip of his cigar around in the fire floating in front of his face.

"Thank you, Bradley."

The butler extinguished the large cedar match and then left the room.

The combination of the ancient spirit and the lit Gurkha Black Dragon cigar filled his nostrils with vanilla and warm, toasted caramel.

His guests sat talking among themselves. He walked from the window into the ornately decorated study. His bookshelves were covered with masterworks from Tolstoy, Mark Twain, and P. G. Woodhouse. He even had in a case an original 1897 Fitzgerald translation of *Rubáiyát of Omar Khayyám*.

He walked to the front of the fireplace.

"Friends, thank you so much for making the long journey to my humble home. I hope the amenities are to your liking. What I have brought you here to discuss is what should be done about this organization that none of you have seem to have heard of before. This Arrangements by Ariel situation has caused our investors and partners to clam up. Over the last month, every resource we can bring to bear has been studying their locations and personnel around the globe. We even kidnapped one of theirs from Pakistan earlier last month, and do you know what happened?"

Everyone in the room looked at him blankly.

"We got nothing. He died of a heart attack. Isn't that convenient. Friends, you especially, Mr. Secretary, we need these bunglers neutered at worst, strung up and flayed at best. I want their phone networks, their server locations. I want to know where Ariel is. We sent two kill teams after her and her little bartender friend, and do you know what we have received for our efforts?"

The powerful men in the room remained silent.

"Sixty dead mercenaries who have handled countless jobs harder than this one for us for years. Edward was a good man who had our vision at heart, a godly man. But Edward got sloppy. Our new fixer, Mr. Zarov, here will not be so careless in the future."

Marquis raised his glass in a small toast and gave Aldrich a slight nod.

The secretary of defense cleared his throat loudly to indicate it was his turn to talk. "Aldrich, we have run smoke screens for our operation that is currently pending in Nigeria. When can we expect the mining rights to be signed over? This was due a month ago, and it feels like we are just sitting on our hands."

Aldrich nodded and walked over to a computer situated off to the side. "I thought you may bring that up. In your e-mail inbox, when you have time to view, it will be an e-mail. Attached to that e-mail is a PDF with the entire charter signed and executed by President Buhari, who is very excited about the new understanding that he has with the United States of America. The original document is on its way to your office now. This is the part where you thank our dear Mr. Zarov."

Marquis smiled at the politician and nodded his head. The secretary of defense was obviously now deeply on the back foot.

"Well, you continue to impress, Mr. Alecto. I will get you anything you need on whoever this person or persons is. Please pass all the intel you have to my secretary."

Aldrich Alecto was a man accustomed to getting what he wanted, but the showmanship of this moment still excited him.

"Well, sir, I do my best to under promise and over deliver."

The secretary stood and shook Aldrich's hand. "I think we are going to continue to do great things together, Mr. Alecto."

Aldrich smiled back at the aging statesman. "More things that have been dreamt of in heaven or earth, Mr. Secretary."

The secretary clinked Aldrich's glass, and the statesman proposed a toast. "To Christendom."

The men around him echoed the toast. "To Christendom."

A man with a scar on his face in the corner remained silent.

The secretary departed the study, which now only had Aldrich, Marquis Zarov, and two intelligence chiefs from Washington—to whom he now turned his attention.

"Gentleman, you both represent a massive percentage of Americas covert capabilities. I assume that, with the secretary's blessing, you will be capable of helping us with our little problem."

The man in the corner who had a massive scar that ran up his neck across his nose and ended on his forehead spoke. "Yes, sir, the special activities center has been sucking up data since you brought this to our attention, and we have an idea of what this is. But, unfortunately, at this time, the information we need is locked inside of a special-access program that appears to have no director. Or rather, hasn't had a director since 1994. With that in mind, we are currently running down all known individuals associated with the organization. The program is not tied to any agency or oversight. It is deep black. Which means that it's not a matter of it being a secret. It is a matter of no one knowing what question to ask."

Aldrich nodded, deep in thought. "Is it possible she works for the government in an official capacity?"

The man with the scar laughed. "Um. No, sir. If she did, it would be a simple matter for us to track down her information and handle this internally. But there is nothing in her file classified or otherwise that would lead us to believe that she has ever worked for or applied for a government position. I mean, hell, we would need to pay her somehow, and there is nothing not a single trace of ties to any government entity. The closest thing to government involvement is, she personally made some of the flower arrangements for the White House correspondence dinner a few years back. We had a few of our guys break into the headquarters in Seattle, and it is completely gutted, absolutely nothing there to trace where she went or what the organization is really doing."

Aldrich took a pull off the masterpiece of a cigar and let the smoke float out of his mouth.

"I see. Well, you just gave me an idea. Marquis, call your friend at the IRS and see if you can get their tax records released."

Marquis took a puff off his cigar and nodded, pulling out his phone to text his friend at the IRS.

Aldrich looked satisfied. "Okay, so the team that was sent in, is there anything that could tie them back to us or the projects we are working on?"

Zarov shook his head "No. We hired through our normal channels, and we liquidated the middlemen. There is no link. However, some of the men that were on the op have worked for us in the past."

Zarov nodded. "Best to assume I think that they already know who we are. No reason to assume our opponent is playing chess in the dark."

Everyone in the room nodded at this. Aldrich continued to give orders out.

"Mr. Director, if you would be so kind, my companion here has a few things he will be needing from you within the next week. Please stay and hear him out. I have a flight that leaves in two hours and must go. You are all welcome to the estate and all its amenities. Please let Bradley know if you need anything, and I do mean anything. You will find Bradley, I think, most resourceful."

Aldrich started from the room, a satisfied smug smile on his face. He mused to himself, "By God's grace, the work continues. To him be the glory."

— *Chapter 27* —

Montenegro

TWENTY-FOUR HOURS LATER, I arrived at Tivat Airport in Montenegro. I moved from the plane onto the steps leading down onto the tarmac. Waiting for me on the Tarmac was a black car and, to my utter astonishment because she had said nothing, my girlfriend.

Ariel was in a white flowing sundress, holding in her hand a little sign on it that said, "Asshole."

I laughed and fast-walked through the crowd of people over to her. I scooped her up in a hug and felt her body press up against mine for the first time in a month. Her little sign clattered to the ground. Being this close to her caused a bunch of pent-up feelings to come. But she was laughing as I spun her, so I pushed complicated thoughts to the side and simply reveled in the moment. I kissed her hard, trying to pour every minute we were apart into that kiss.

"My goodness, sir, did you miss me that much?"

"You have no idea."

She pecked me on the nose and said, "Did you learn anything?"

"I am much scarier than I was a month ago."

She nodded and said icily, "Good. You are going to need it. We are moving on Zarov and Alecto tomorrow night. We found them. They are less than twelve miles from where you are standing right now."

I smiled, feeling my anger stir, asking for release. Hearing one of my trainers from Tampa in my mind, "Anger is a gift, but as an emotion, it isn't useful for the person wielding the tool of violence. Hate, on the other hand, hate is priceless."

I let the anger pass, but the hate that came behind—that I focused on and fed.

Ariel snapped me out of my internal monologue. "Come on, sexy, we need to get on the road. The team is waiting on us."

"Feather or heart."

She smiled, saying back the customary reply, "We balance the scales. Get in the damn car."

We rode toward the city of Budva. The curving coastal road opened onto a bay that the sun had started to sink into. The view took my breath away. The stunning azure of the ocean interplayed, reflecting the sun's flickering rays. Ariel's thumb was tracing little figure eights on the back of my hand when a thought seemed to strike her. She reached into a bag at her feet.

She said, "I, um, got you something."

She handed me a velvet box that looked like a box you kept a ring in.

My eyes went wide, and I smiled. "Um, yes."

A punch landed on my arm. "Stupid."

I took the box and opened it. It was the same necklace that Ariel had on. A simple silver dagger on a thin silver chain. I smiled and looked deep into Ariel's piercing green eyes. There I saw a soul that matched mine perfectly, one that loved me despite the catastrophe of our shared existence. In those eyes laid promise, hope, and a future that I could not help but long for.

"I am…overwhelmed. Thank you."

She smiled and kissed me on the cheek.

"You are welcome, my sweet man. The dagger on the chain is a Fairbairn–Sykes fighting dagger. It was the preferred tool of the OSS when things got a little too up close and personal. It is a reminder that you must fight however you can no matter how unfair. Honor belongs to the dead. Also, it means I love you and stuff, but don't read too much into it."

I smiled, knowing her predilection for underselling things. "Wouldn't dream of it."

I put on the necklace, feeling like I had just given a promise ring.

We pulled into the headquarters of the Montenegrin Arrangements by Ariel, which, to my surprise, was small and quaint in comparison to the large monolith that was their Seattle location.

Another surprise hit me as we went in through the front gate. The sign on the front of the building said, "Arrangements by Dmitri."

"Who the fuck is Dmitri?"

Ariel smiled. "All of our locations abroad have the name of their CEO on the business. They have everything we have in Seattle, minus the moot. And Azrael has jurisdiction over all."

I nodded my understanding, and the gate security guard, who I noticed was an Azrael agent, opened the gate and let us through.

Chapter 28

Dmitri

We unloaded the car with my duffel bag and backpack. Ariel was noticeably quiet as we walked to the front entrance of what looked like an old Roman church that had been converted into a house. She walked to the front door, and a suit-clad Azrael agent opened the door for us.

We stepped into a colorful lobby, which was decorated with the most beautiful flower arrangements I had ever seen. They lined the walls, free standing in massive vases and hanging from the ceiling like a cornucopia of color and texture. I recognized the Kadupul flower making an appearance here and there; dragon lilies, roses, and orchids of every shape and size. In the middle of the rotund lobby was a giant red flower I had never seen before. It had a massive hole in the middle, and it had to be at least three feet wide.

I whispered to Ariel, "What is that thing?"

Ariel smiled. "One of Dr. Isley's creations. That is the Rafflesia arnoldii elysium. It's slightly smaller, unmodified cousin is commonly called the corpse flower. Before you ask, it's because it smells like death. This one smell and tastes like honeysuckle. The original flower is a parasite that grows on vines in the Amazon. We grow a massive knot of honeysuckle and then let this guy grow on top of it. One of our bestsellers."

I was in awe of the massive plant when a very tall man that had long, dark hair and a long, scraggly black beard walked into the room next to a vacant receptionist desk.

He looked at Ariel long and hard for a moment and, in one of the thickest Russian accents I'd ever heard, said, "Why do we not speak of death?"

Ariel smiled and stepped forward. "Because death, like life, happens without our permission."

Dmitri smiled wide and held his arms out. "Welcome to Montenegro, Vidar. All of our assets are at your disposal, as am I."

Ariel stepped forward to shake the man's hand. "It is very nice to meet you in person, Dmitri. My father speaks very fondly of his time with you."

Dmitri's smile widened. "How is the old crow? I have not heard from him since my wedding a few years ago."

Ariel pulled out of her bag a velvet case and spoke, "He is very well, and he sends this gift with his kindest regards." Ariel handed the case to Dmitri, who cracked it open, and his eyes went wide.

"How is it possible that you have brought me this?"

Ariel smiled wide. "Othan wanted you to have the final piece of your 1911 collection. He knew that this was one that you could not possibly have yet. Lou Biondo made this one himself."

Dmitri looked overwhelmed. "May I?"

Ariel nodded enthusiastically. "Of course, it is yours."

Dmitri pulled out a perfectly strange, beautifully engraved, gray-in-color 1911 handgun. It looked like it was something out of a comic book. Dmitri held it carefully, like a newborn baby. He slowly pulled the magazine free and racked the guns slide. A round came flying out, which he deftly caught in midair.

"Othan never did like a gun that was unloaded," the older Russian man mused at the priceless art piece. "Made from a meteorite older than our planet, and now it is in my hand. Incredible. Who is your friend here, Ariel?"

Ariel motioned me forward. "This is Sammi. He is my boyfriend. He just graduated our school in Tampa."

Dmitri smiled and shook my hand. "And in which order did these two titles bestow themself on you, Sammi? I only joke. To business?"

Ariel nodded. "That would be most helpful."

Dmitri motioned them toward the alcove behind the receptionist's desk. "Come. Your team waits for you."

With seemingly no prompt, the wall behind the receptionist's desk lit with the scales of Anubis inlaid in the wall and then slid apart soundlessly.

The internal structure of the building did nothing to persuade me that it had not been a church at one time. The ornate carvings on the columns looked ancient. Little flowers and vines had been carved into them. The vast, stained-glass window at the back of the interior depicted the scales of Anubis shattering the illusion.

He motioned us through the room full of workers going about their daily tasks to a conference room off to the right. Opening the door, light spilled out, as well as a few familiar voices. Doc, Phill, Petra, Eli, Rook, and Bobby were all standing around the table, looking at a map and a large-scale model of the city of Budva.

"If we set up here, 40 percent of the approach is blind."

They looked up, and Ariel said, "Anybody know where I can find some real tier-one killers and a decent bottle of whiskey?"

They all smiled.

Doc said, "Hey, boss. Long time no see."

Phill nodded to me. I returned the gesture. Ariel stepped to the middle of the group.

Petra said, "Good to have you back, boss."

Ariel gave her a sidelong look. "Oh, you liked having extra time with your big slab of meat over there. Don't pretend like you missed me."

Petra laughed, but turned red and said nothing.

"Alright then. Everyone's here. Let's work up a plan."

— Chapter 29 —

Zarov

Marquis rolled over in the massive, Alaskan, king-sized bed. The previous night's debauchery rolled over him as his hangover set in.

He noticed that there were still three girls asleep in his bed. His first thought was to scream at them to fuck off, but he restrained himself. Mostly because the extra noise would add to his misery. Remembering he had a meeting later in the day with a local mafia boss to secure some extra talent, he grabbed his phone.

There were several alerts on his Signal app, which he took as a good sign, but didn't open them yet. The ornate bedroom had just started to glow with the early morning sunrise when a knock at the door roused him from his groggy thoughts.

Bradley, the butler, stuck his head in the room and said audibly but quietly, "Sir, there is a man here to see you. He says you two were friends from grammar school."

This startled him, but he was awake now. He swung his legs out of the bed, and one of the Russian whores in his bed moved and groaned, stretching herself awake.

"Good morning, lover. How did you sleep?"

Marquis did not respond.

She nuzzled up against him, and he thought to himself, *This was power*.

He spoke, "Why are you just lying there? Come over here and suck my dick."

She complied without a word. Bradley, embarrassed, turned red when he saw this and started to leave.

"And where are you going?"

Zarov asked as he slapped the asses of the other two women who woke and squealed at his unkind touch. "Go over there and take care of our friend, Bradley."

Bradley put his hands up, trying to retreat from the room, but Marquis said in words cold as death, "I wasn't asking."

Bradley stopped frozen and, with reluctance, accepted the situation. The girls went over and began doing what they were told.

"He can wait for a few minutes in the lobby, don't you think, Bradley?"

The butler looked like his soul was being removed from his body.

"Y-yes, sir."

Marquis laid back and let the Russian girl do her job. He mused, *This is what power should be. Any desire you have instantly fulfilled the instant you have it.*

Bradley was making some less-than-dignified sounds. Another thought flitted through Marquis's quagmire of a brain. *You should make him fuck the whores.*

Marquis sat up, the girl pausing, letting him adjust himself.

He noticed the wedding ring on Bradley's hand; this gave him no pause.

"Bradley, bring your girls up here on the bed and fuck them for me, will you."

Bradley started to protest, but remembered that this was a life-or-death situation, and it was best to just comply. Marquis smiled as Bradley slid into one of the prostitutes, who either felt pleasure or feigned it. Marquis grabbed the prostitute's head and choked her as he finished. He sighed and pushed the girl off him.

"Okay, Bradley, finish up. We have company."

Bradley did as he was told.

Minutes after the fivesome, Marquis and Bradley made their way to the front foyer, where a tall man with long black hair and a scraggly beard was waiting for him. Marquis came down the long staircase, smiling as he descended.

"Dmitri, how are you today?"

The large man smiled and held his hands wide.

"I can't complain. Life is good, my friend."

Marquis hugged the man and kissed him on each cheek. "What brings you to me today?"

Dmitri smiled and pulled out a piece of paper and handed it to him.

Marquis read the piece of paper. "Tonight? And these are their plans?"

Dmitri nodded. "Just as I promised. Now where is what I was promised."

Marquis smiled and said, "Bradley, there is a suitcase in the other room. Bring it to me please."

Bradley departed.

"If I may ask, tovarich, why turn on your companions? I mean, I know the money is important to you, but what is the real reason."

Dmitri's countenance turned serious. "The bitch in charge thinks she can just walk into my house and do anything that she wants. Well, I think this time tomorrow that will no longer be an issue for me. Also, I think that she would frown on me working with and sometimes for outsiders. This solves both problems."

Bradley returned with a suitcase and handed it to Marquis.

"Well, I hope for both our sakes, we don't see each other again."

Dmitri extended his hand, and Marquis shook it. "I am sure that we won't, friend. We are far too cautious for such things."

Marquis handed the suitcase to Dmitri, saying, "Dosvedonya."

Dmitri nodded his head in respect, saying, "Dosvedonya, my friend."

Dmitri walked out the front door of the estate, where a black car and a driver was waiting for him.

Marquis smiled. All those CIA assets paid off and got him some actionable intel. He opened his cell phone and looked at the Signal app. Five of his best shooters had landed that morning and had set up shop in a hotel a few miles away. He made a group message and sent the address of the estate to his men, following it up with, *Be here in one hour.*

He pocketed the cell phone, satisfied.

"Bradley."

The butler clearly looked uncomfortable. "Yes, sir."

"How about you and I go back in the bedroom and see if those sluts have a little more in them?"

Bradley shifted from one foot to another. "Yes, sir."

Marquis smiled, knowing that this would be the lowest form of pleasure he would experience today. There was nothing quite like killing an enemy who was trying to kill you.

He mused to himself, *What was it Hemingway said? Those who have hunted armed men long enough and liked it never care much for anything else thereafter.*

Marquis had hunted armed and unarmed men and women the world over for over a decade now, and for him, nothing was quite so sweet as the hunt. Today, today was special though. Today he got to hunt an apex predator. Marquis was quite satisfied with the day he had planned for himself as Bradley led the way back to the bedroom and awaiting hookers.

— Chapter 30 —

The Short Drop

I SAT IN THE conference room after making myself a cup of coffee. I sipped the black coffee and reflected deeply over the last few months of my life. B-Don whispered from my memories, "You aren't dead yet, buddy. Make sure you keep getting better."

I remembered how much I liked bartending. Maybe when everything was said and done, Ariel and I could buy a bar and run it. We could call it Feather or Heart. Othan's words were an ever-present reminder: "You will never find peace that lasts." The weight of all that I had become made me confident, but as everyone came back into the conference room, for the first time in a long time, something that felt rotten entered my mind—fear. Fear that I would fail. Fear of the unknown. Fear, that I would die or that Ariel would die. I held the complicated cocktail of emotions in my mind. Ariel pulled me from my reverie.

"You okay?"

"I...am afraid."

Ariel pursed her lips. "Good. Fear before a mission means you aren't crazy."

I nodded, accepting this truth. "And I am thinking about B-Don."

Ariel smiled. "Have you ever heard of the Maori Ttibe from New Zealand?"

I shrugged. "I have."

Ariel plowed ahead. "They have a belief in the balance of things, much as we do. They called what we are doing here today, Taua Roto. Most people think it means revenge. But its true translation is, 'the maintenance of balance.' Which is it you are after today? Is it revenge? Or balance?"

I looked away, afraid tears would come. "I am after both."

Everyone had gathered back together after planning into the early morning and sleeping in until 11:00 a.m. local time.

Petra and Rook seemed to really be hanging on every word the other said; the thought made me smile. Imagine the babies they would have.

Ariel came to the head of the table. "Everyone happy with the plan?"

Everyone nodded, and no one spoke.

"Alright then. Take it easy today. I mean it. I want everyone napping, snoozing, and otherwise conserving mind and body. Dmitri, is our tertiary extract in place?"

Dmitri nodded. "Yes, Vidar, all assets have confirmed. They are green and standing by."

Ariel nodded. "Bobby, talk to me about our jammer."

He said, "Three AI-controlled drones will prevent any camera or cell phones from getting footage of us. We also have a diversion that a few locals are going to help us generate to keep local LE response time high."

I had a thought. "If Zarov and Alecto are not in the car, what do we do?"

"Good question. The plan does not change. If he isn't in the car, then we follow the extract plan. Any questions on any other mission specifics?" Ariel looked around the room, waiting.

No one spoke. The operators all stood.

She smiled at each of them in turn. "Feather or heart."

The words took on a new weight for me, like a sacred mantra muttered by monks.

"We balance the scales!"

Everyone filed out of the room and went their own way.

Phill put a hand on my shoulder. "You ready for this, buddy? It's your first one, so you are basically still a potato. I would understand if you were afraid of being deep-fried."

I shook my head. "I don't know, man. I am not sure if you are ever ready for anything. You just tuck your chin and try not to freak out."

"Well, that was the right answer. Killing is kind of like sex. You have no idea how it really works the first time, and you feel really guilty for no particular reason afterward."

Doc laughed. "I have never felt guilty after killing someone."

Phill snorted. "I know, but that is because you need professional care from a mental health physician."

"And you don't?"

Phill smiled with a twinkle in his eye "Well, that's different. I have abused my well-being so badly that I came full circle and returned to normal."

Ariel walked over. "Hey, Sammi, while you're all here, there is something you need to see."

She turned on the conference rooms projector, and I saw her google CNBC Arrangements by Ariel CCO interview.

Phill turned red and exclaimed. "Don't you fucking dare. I will go get Snuggles right goddamn now."

Ariel smiled as she playfully waved the remote like a magic wand. "Well, you could, but I will have already played it by the time you get back."

Phill crossed his arms and pouted.

Several YouTube videos popped up in the result, but she played the one uploaded a week ago. Unlike Phill's normal attire of 5.11 shirts and liquor-company T-shirts, he was wearing a tailored black suit and smart-looking, businessman-style glasses.

The TV anchor asked him, "Phill, Arrangements by Ariel on paper is a company that sources and sells flowers, but you are not a florist. Explain to me and the viewers how a florist company is worth over a billion dollars."

Phill smiled into the camera and leaned toward the anchorman. "Well, Robert, that is a good question. Our company is not, in fact, as you put it, a florist company. We are an applied science and software company. Our software is used by almost every florist on the planet to connect customers with them instantly. That is our market value.

We are the Amazon of flower arrangements. And our applied-science division that was started twenty years ago diversifies our portfolio."

The anchor nodded. "So what is this recent headquarters move your company has undertaken? Should shareholders be worried?"

Phill laughed good-naturedly. "No, Robert, our shareholders have nothing to be concerned about. Our CEO, as you know, is a little eccentric at times, but her leadership has brought us to heights her great-grandfather could not have possibly imagined. This move is simply her way of bringing focus back to the land and our roots. We have moved to one of our largest farms in the southern part of Mexico for a couple reasons. Number one, the disparity between the corporate side of our business and the farming side is something that bothers Ariel greatly. She thinks that if you work hard, you should be able to earn a living wage for you and your family, so she has committed to building an entire city around our farms in the southern part of Mexico, with schools, restaurants, movie theaters, hospitals, the works. Her theory is that if we can create internally consistent places for our employees to live their lives in, then we don't have to consider the impact because they will be spending their hard-earned money with us instead of letting those resources fall into the hands of the corrupt governments that rule the places we outsource our labor too."

The anchor looked like he had bitten a sour grape. "What are you trying to say here, Phill? Correct me if I'm wrong, but is Ariel building a utopia for the downtrodden and deserving poor?"

Phill shook his head. "No, she is just trying to be able to sleep at night. Do you think that Apple or Nike have considered the needs of those that work in their sweatshops in China or Taiwan? How about the suicide nets they must string around their factories to prevent workers from jumping to their death? What if they used some of those profits to reinvest in their workforce? Do you think their brand would have less blood on it if their cobalt mines or their lithium mines had basic health care provided? Or if their workers could easily afford to feed themselves and their families? How about these multibillion-dollar companies stop colluding with foreign governments to steal natural resources from people that rely on them to survive?"

Robert clearly wasn't ready for this type of response. "Phill, I am sure you aren't saying that Apple and Nike are evil?"

Phill took a breath. "Yes, I am saying that. You can make money and care about the people that are letting you make money off them at the same time."

Ariel shook her head and turned off the video. Ariel laughed and shook her head. "And that's the story of how our stock dropped eight points in one day."

Phill said, "Psh, it will recover in like a month, and we can use the nonprofit to publicize our way out of it. Also, they can all fuck off. I'm right."

Ariel shook her head slowly. "We literally kill some of the fuckers that put people in those positions. Do you think that is not enough of an extreme measure?"

Doc chimed in, "Well, I think it's nice we are standing up for the little guy. Makes me feel all warm and fuzzy. Now that my drinking ban is over, can I get hammered, please?"

Ariel smiled. "Now? No. After? Yes."

Doc cracked his knuckles. "Titties, let's get this done then."

The day passed slowly, like waiting to go to the principal's office. Ariel and I lounged by the pool for a bit and then went inside to our bedroom and took a nap. We awoke at 5:00 p.m. local time and readied ourselves for war. Outside there were three local vehicles that had been configured for our use, one utility van that said on the side in stylized letters, "Aranžmani Dmitri." This was the van that Doc, Phill, and I loaded into.

I put my large duffel bag and a rifle case into the van, and off we went into the old city.

Zarov had no idea what was coming for him. In my pocket was B-Don's cigarette case full of American spirits and his Zippo lighter. I played with the lighter, thinking about B-Don and what Zarov did to him. I would smoke one of these cigarettes over his dead body and avenge my friend. I personally did not believe in a God or afterlife, but in this moment, I didn't really care. I whispered a quite thought to my late friend.

"Hey, buddy. Only one more move on the board. We are going to send this guy to whatever afterlife you are in so you can kick his ass for eternity. Thank you for pulling me out of the gutter when no one else cared. I wish you could meet Ariel. She is really something. See you soon."

— *Chapter 31* —

And a Sudden Stop

I HAD REVIEWED A picture of Alecto and Zarov, but I had HITA put them in the top-left corner of my HUD just in case. I also asked him to check in with Ariel when a convenient moment arose.

I sighted down the scope of my .408 CheyTac Intervention. The rifle was something I had trained heavily with while I was at Tampa, and the Nightforce NXS 8-32x56mm scope reticle danced over the curve in the road. The curve was small in the artificially lit night. I checked my range finder again. 855 yards.

The flower van was parked on the left side of the road from my vantage, right at the curve's apex. Small street vendors and people on bicycles went about their lives none the wiser at what was about to happen.

Ariel spoke over the comm as they waited, "Why the fuck did I just get a call from Snoop Dog?"

"Sammi, what the fuck?" Doc mumbled.

I laughed as did Phill.

HITA responded on the open comm, "Bitch, don't act like you aren't impressed. Your helmet was busy playing solitaire, and I configured and collated all the drone footage so your silly self would have a countdown when the vehicles come into effective range, but don't worry 'bout that. I'm shuttin' up."

"Oh shit," I exclaimed.

"Clear comms," Ariel snapped.

We fell silent.

"TOC, this is Dagger Actual. All elements are in position."

Skuld's voice came over the channel. "Good copy, Dagger."

My breathing was slow and steady.

Phill, who was positioned two buildings away from me, said, "Do you really think Alecto will be in the car as well, Vidar?"

Ariel responded, "Doesn't matter. Focus."

Twenty minutes passed as the evening gave way to the moonless night.

Doc and Ariel were stationed in a nondescript sedan about ten yards behind the flower van. I moved my reticle up and saw a little black quadcopter drone floating about three hundred feet in the air above the road.

"TOC to Dagger Actual, vehicles are approaching five hundred yards out at approximately thirty-five miles per hour."

"Good copy, TOC."

Ariel's voice came over the radio again a few seconds later. "Fifteen seconds out. I have control."

The two black sedans rolled around a blind curve and then began moving slowly toward their doom. I aligned my body to the spot in the road that I had sighted on and put into my ballistics computer.

The bumper of the sedan came into view, and I took up slack in the incredibly light trigger.

The driver's side of the second vehicle slid into view.

"Execute."

My crosshair was placed right at the top of where the steering wheel would be. I knew from my training that the bullet would angle slightly up as it hit the glass. As the last syllable left Ariel's mouth, I slowly felt myself reach my natural respiratory pause and pressed the trigger ever so gently to the rear.

The explosion from my round pushed the curtains that were partially closed out the open window. Simultaneously the van holding the small but incredibly specific bomb went off, sending a three-pound chunk of copper that had recently turned to a molten spear directly through the first vehicle's engine block. I ran the bolt on my rifle back home and put another round in the second vehicle's engine block as it screeched to a halt.

I immediately pulled myself off the table and collapsed the rifle. A moment later, I heard a thwack.

The table where I was laying moments before had a leg blown off, and now it sank a tripod rather than a table.

That was not part of the plan.

"Dagger 3, Dagger 7. Contact. Sniper unknown direction."

As soon as she called the shot, Ariel and Doc leapt from their hide vehicle, rifles in hand. They slid their helmets on and moved toward the immobile vehicles.

People were screaming and running in every direction.

Perfect, she thought to herself as she came to the back door of the second vehicle. She shot through the glass multiple times and pushed the glass in with the muzzle of her rifle.

She investigated the hole she had made and saw one man slumped over the steering wheel, with no one else inside. Doc did the same and checked the front seat.

Doc came up, his rifle moving to low ready. "Nothing, boss. Dry hole."

A shot rang out, and this set Ariel in motion.

"It's a counter ambush. All elements move to—" Ariel's world turned black.

I ran down the stairs, moving to support the ambushed interdiction force as they fought their way out of the kill zone. My trainer's words in my ears were screaming. "You are being ambushed. If you are alive to have this thought, you have already survived it. To continue surviving it, the first thing to do is get off the X."

I heard another shot ring out and heard Phill say calmly, "Dagger Actual is down. I repeat, Dagger Actual is down."

I shed my helmet and my armor as I ran down the flight of stairs. My heart redlined. Ariel was down. *It's okay. Doc is with her. She's fine. Everything is fine.*

Knowing that the strange alienlike gear would do nothing but expose me as a target in the crowd of people, I inserted an earpiece into my ear so that I could be on comms without my helmet.

"Location on the shooter?"

The TOC replied, "755 yards to your right, eighth floor, grey building, Dagger 7."

Phill spoke, "I have him."

A boom reverberated off the walls of the ancient city.

"He's down. There is probably at least one more."

I ran out the front of the building, and in the distance, I heard another rifle crack. Phill had moved locations and expertly sighted in on the other shooter with a little help from their drone asset.

"I have the position of the other shooter, but he is moving. Going to wait for him to settle."

A moment later, Phill's .408 spoke again. The other shooter was no longer a problem.

Petra's voice broke over the comm. "Fuck, there is another shooter. Maybe more than one just took accurate fire."

As I exited the front door of the building, I saw a guy with a scooter. I grabbed a large bottle of water off a table and threw it at the man's head, knocking him from his Vespa.

I picked up the scooter and tore as fast as the little motor would allow toward the sight of the ambush. Images of Ariel in our little hideaway on the fifty-fourth floor came unbidden to my mind's eye. I banished them with a curse. The Vespa was faster than Ol'bessy had been, and in my haste, I almost laid down the small scooter. I gunned the throttle of the small machine, and it screamed, reaching its top speed.

Crack. A round zipped past my head and exploded on the brick road to my left. Panic started to build. *In for four, hold for four, out for four, pause for four.*

You are going to lose her just like you lost B-Don.

"Shut the fuck up," I said out loud to myself.

"Directional mics report two shooters in proximity. Church tower to the east. Assuming control of drone one." Petra's calculated speech was the drone of death's choir.

Bobby spoke like an auctioneer. "Three-pound payload, Petra. Park it in the middle or the whole building could come down."

Petra keyed her mic, acknowledging the information. She hurtled the drone at our would-be executioner and pushed the button.

A boom and a puff of smoke in the church tower was the death knell for the rest of the ambushers.

As I arrived, I saw Ariel. She had taken a round from the snipers to the helmet.

My heart sank, and I began to panic. "Not now, you little bitch," I told myself. "She needs you. Do not let her down."

Doc carefully slid her helmet off, and this made me start crying, but I stifled it.

There was a massive wound on the right side of her face. Part of her right cheek was missing, and blood gushed from the wound.

Doc packed her face with gauze and said, "We need to get out of here."

"Dagger, let's fucking move," I commanded.

We loaded into the second van and tore down the road toward Arrangements by Dmitri.

Doc checked Ariel's pulse and said coldly, "When we get there, we are going to kill Dmitri so fucking hard. He sold us out. That is the only way that this could have happened."

I press checked my pistol and spoke, "I need someone to get my armor and rifle. It is in the stairwell in the building.

"On it," Rook replied.

I sat in the floor, holding Ariel's hand.

"Hey, baby. It's going to be okay. They have a medical facility where we are going. Doc?"

I looked up into Doc's face, and his mouth drew a tight line. He mouthed, "I don't know. It's bad."

I nodded. Looking back down at Ariel, tears stung my eyes, threating to reduce me to sobbing. I shoved it down as deep as I could—deep where the cancer grows.

We were three minutes from the front gate of Arrangements by Dmitri when Ariel began to breath in short, explosive, and gurgling gasps.

Doc checked her airway, and it was clear, so he started an IV.

He said, "She has a collapsed lung. Eli, how far out are we?"

Eli turned in the passenger seat with one finger raised.

Doc nodded. "Skuld, are they ready for us?"

The comm crackled. "Confirmed, Dagger 2."

The gate was open when we arrived, and a full complement of medical personnel were waiting on us. We stepped out of the van, and they took Ariel immediately into the medical ward.

I went with her until a woman put a kind hand on my arm and said in broken, Russian-accent-laden English, "You can't come any further. We have her."

I stood and watched them wheel her into a side entrance and disappear.

── *Chapter 32* ──

Served Cold

As the rest of Dagger began to take stock, Doc looked at me with menace in his eyes. "Sammi?"

I nodded.

"Phill?"

Phill nodded and press-checked his rifle.

"Okay then. Let's get this fucker," Doc said with a predator's grin.

I press-checked my SIG P320 and checked that my Microtech Halo VI was still in my pocket. We went through the front door of Arrangements by Dmitri and cleared our way methodically through the front lobby of the building.

A new voice came over the comm. "Sammi, do you copy?"

I stopped and said, "Yes."

"This is Archangel. I oversee the Azrael. Dmitri is in his office, and he is waiting for you. You should meet no armed resistance."

"Doc, we are clear all the way."

He nodded, and we ran to Dmitri's office at the back of the complex.

Doc and I kicked the door in to see a calm Dmitri sitting at his desk.

"Friends, welcome. Did your adventure not go as planned?"

I holstered my Sig. Phill did not remove his rifle from his shoulder. Neither did Doc.

Dmitri smiled. "What? You know I was right. Ariel is leading us down an impossible path. In the public eye, but still running things like it's 1946? No. I could not allow this. If we would have continued with her in charge, then what? We eventually get found out and tried for war crimes? Disavowed by all of the governments that our actions prop up. Or do we expect the international community to simply say, 'Oh well, they are only killing the bad guys. That's fine.' When did they vote for us? When did they decide this is what they want? They didn't."

Dmitri took a bottle of vodka from a chilling bucket and poured himself a shot, throwing it back.

"You know that the guy you are after is eventually either going to kill you all or—"

I pulled the knife from my pocket and jumped onto Dmitri's large desk.

The trademark shick sound came from the large blade. I flipped it around into a hammer grip as I descended on the large Russian man.

His hands came up to defend himself, but my action had taken him by surprise. I plunged the knife into his face, shredding through one of his hands in the process.

The rolling high-backed chair fell backward with our momentum. As we hit the floor, we landed, with me in mount. I stabbed him in the face over and over, feeling the knife hit his cheekbone, then the corner of his eye socket, then his forehead. I flipped the knife into standard grip. I stabbed him in the chest, feeling every impact shred the last vestiges of my humanity. Dmitri screamed like a hyena as my blade did its grizzly work. I then switched to his abdomen and stabbed repeatedly, the blind rage and hatred free-flowing into my shoulder's arms and hands. He fought helplessly to grab the hand that was sending the knife into him like a sowing machine. For a moment, I felt the knife embed in his chest, and I could feel his heartbeat through the blade. Blood coated my face and my hands, but I didn't stop. I stabbed him again, sinking the knife into the side of his neck, pulling the knife back toward me in a sawing motion. I then sawed back down, feeling bone. I grabbed the knife with two hands. Finding the joint, I sawed through it. Dimitris's head came free from his neck with a sickening sound.

Doc walked over, pulling me off the desecrated body.

"Oosa, little demon, oosa. You got him."

Only then did I realize the extent of what I had done. I looked down at my work, and it looked like Dmitri had been torn apart by a wild animal. I realized as an afterthought that this was exactly what happened.

Phill looked on and whistled. "Well, that was metal as fuck."

Doc laughed. "I know. The only reason I stopped him was, my dick can't get any harder."

Phill laughed, but I was blank and quiet. "Maybe we can Eiffel Tower the head. I am only joking if you aren't down."

I was still angry. The demented conversation in the background faded from my ears as I looked down at the mayhem I had wrought. I looked at what had once been a face on a head that used to be Dmitri, and I felt nothing. Then as my adrenaline faded, the boy that I had been seemed to speak from the darkness.

No more pencils, no more books. You killed me when you killed him.

I sat on the edge of Dmitri's desk and saw the velvet box containing the priceless 1911 that Othan had sent him. I opened the case and put the 1911 in my waistband after clearing the round from the chamber and reinserting the magazine.

"Taking souvenirs? He's a natural-born killer." Doc remarked like I wasn't there.

"I mean, look at Dmitri. The dude was bound to drop rare loot," Phill responded.

I walked from the room in a daze, Dmitri's blood still covering me. I pressed the earpiece in my ear and said, "Skuld, it's Sammi. How is Ariel?"

Chapter 33

Nihil Vivit Aut Frustra Moritur

Zarov waved and snaped his fingers. A waiter made his way quickly to his table.

"Can we have another bottle of the 1975 Domaine Leflaive Chevalier-Montrachet Grand Cru?"

The waiter said, "Of course, monsieur. Restaurant policy requires me to tell you that the bottle is fourteen-hundred Euros."

Zarov nodded and waved the man away dismissively as if he needed to hear the price. The beautiful French girl across from Zarov swooned at the price tag of the wine.

"Well, if you are willing to spend that on a bottle of wine, maybe you could extend your stay for a week or two. Let me show you a really good time?"

Zarov smiled, appreciating the businesswoman's nose for more money on the table.

"Unfortunately, tonight is the last night I will be here in the city of lights. My work draws me elsewhere."

The girl showed disappointment, but like every other emotion other than the interest in money, it was feigned. Unlike the Eastern European whores, this one was an independent contractor. Zarov preferred it that way. He liked his sex to be as transactional as renting a car. With as many complications.

A few minutes later, their food arrived. He had ordered the duck fois gras. She, much to his suspicion, had simply picked the most expensive thing the menu had to offer. And indeed, it was a lobster tail the size of a baby covered in caviar. They ate the delicious food, and then after another full bottle of wine, Zarov was looking forward to the car ride back to the hotel, where he would take his femme fatale in any way he saw fit.

He snapped his fingers again and waved down their waiter. "We will be skipping dessert."

"No, we won't," his companion said with a wry smile on her face. "I am the dessert."

He handed his card to the waiter, who knowingly moved quickly to get the bill.

Zarov exited and headed for the parking lot directly across the street from the restaurant. He was deeply distrustful of cabs and valets and preferred to park his own car. He also hated cities where having a car was rare. He liked the control his own vehicle gave him.

They got in the elevator and headed for the third floor. Zarov kissed the whore intensely as the elevator rose. The elevator dinged, stilling his passions temporarily. He turned to the door, and as it opened, two things occurred to him at once: there was a 1911 chambered in .45 ACP pointed at his forehead and that he was going to die.

The face above the 1911 cloaked in a hood was one he knew.

"Sammi," he managed past a mouth full of cotton.

I held the custom pistol outside of Zarov's reach, but close enough that he could see the bullet in the chamber. I looked at the call girl.

"Take this bag of money and say nothing of tonight, Appoline."

The girl, shocked to her core at the sound of her real name, reached out. Nodding her acceptance, she took the bag of money.

I looked at my interlocuter with all the desire of a polar bear that was starving.

"Zarov, press the floor 1 button and step out of the elevator."

I could see Zarov thinking about drawing from the drop. I saw him looking for his opportunity. My second hand came up on the gun and the safety came off. This made him recalculate. He complied without a word.

The elevator door closed, leaving us alone in the parking structure. He started to speak.

I cut him off, "With two fingers, take your gun out and throw it over to me."

He did so.

"Now the back up and blade."

He discarded both.

"Before you do this, please know what I did to your friend was not what I wanted to do, Sammi. It's what I had to do. If I wouldn't have given Gallo's boss a body, who do you think he would have come for next?"

I shook my head. "If you want to beg, now would be the time."

He fell to his knees. "I am begging you, please don't do this. I will give you anyone, no, anything you want."

I smiled. "We already know about Alecto. You will be seeing him real soon. I promise you that."

He didn't react, which almost made me hesitate and question him further. But I ignored that impulse. I reached into my pocket and pulled out a black permanent marker. I tossed it to him.

"Mark yourself just like you marked B-Don."

He hesitated and started to say, "Go fuck yourself."

"Do it, or I will go to your mother's nursing home in New York and torture her mercilessly for hours. I will cut her head off with a hacksaw and mail it to your father in Buenos Aries, with the video on a USB drive of the event in her mouth. I swear on my dead friend, I will. Now pick up that marker and do what you were told."

I had no intention of making good on that threat, but the last thing he heard about me was probably what I did to Dmitri. He started crying. I couldn't believe my eyes. He was crying.

He took the marker from the ground and drew an X on his shin and an X on his thigh, and finally, he drew an X on his forehead.

I had dreamed of this moment for the last six months, and finally, this fucker was mine.

"Thank you. You are going to need this in a second."

I tossed him a CAT-T tourniquet. He caught it deftly out of the air, and as his eyes came back to mine, I shot him in the shin. Blood sprayed the concrete under Zarov as the hollow point detonated his calf muscle. After the screaming slowed, I fired again. The round hit

Zarov's thigh, severing his femoral artery the same way he had done to B-Don. Zarov screamed and cursed, but managed to get the tourniquet on his thigh as high up as he could. He cranked the windlass and secured it. He laughed in between screams and then wrote the time on the tourniquet with the black marker.

I smiled and said sweetly, "That was for B-Don."

I started to back away from the wounded man. Horror and hope crossed his face. I could tell he thought this was the end of it. This was the essence of true torment. A glimmer of hope was needed for true despair to set in.

I walked over to the prone man, holstering my now-warm 1911 I pulled out my Microtech. The blade came out as I cut him from the top of his head to the corner of his mouth with a single slash. The wound immediately drew a gush of blood.

"That was for Ariel."

I retracted my knife and slid it into my pocket. Zarov was holding his face, screaming out in pain on the ground next to the elevator.

As Zarov regained his composure, he moaned. "Are we done?"

I shook my head as I walked over to the open trunk of a Mercedes. I smiled at Zarov broadly before revealing what was in my left hand. Out of the truck came a bright-red can of gasoline. His cries for mercy began immediately, but I couldn't hear them. I poured the gas liberally all over the supine figure before me. I remembered the picture of the man from Africa with the tire around his waist—a tire Zarov put there.

He begged, "Please, not like this. No one should have to die like this. Please just shoot me."

"That is the most ironic sentence I have ever heard someone say."

He pointed emphatically to the X on his forehead. "Shoot me. Shoot me!" Zarov cried.

I smiled at him. Reaching in my pocket, I pulled out B-Don's cigarette case and took out an American Spirit. I lit the cigarette using B-Don's Zippo lighter and breathed deep. The smoke burned in my lungs as I let it out. I puffed the cigarette a few more times, adding to the supine man's terror. I watched him contemplate what was about to happen. I drank in every crease and line on his face like a shark eating shipwreck victims. I pulled long and hard on the cancer stick.

"This part is for me."

I flicked the Zippo open and struck it on my pants.

"Catch."

I tossed the lighter, and the man in front of me transformed into a conflagration of screaming, writhing flesh that melted away as he bellowed and breathed the lethal fire into his lungs. His clothes turned to ash, and his hands grabbed at nothing. I stepped back as he tried to crawl toward me. The sound wasn't normal. High-pitched and scathing, it was animalistic and raw. It raked against my ears, and I knew I would hear that scream for the rest of my life. I watched him as he writhed. He slowly stopped screaming and became still.

I picked up the nickel-plated cartridges and put them into my pocket. Smiling at the burning corpse in front of me, I left the garage.

— Chapter 34 —

Peace Everlasting

I stood in front of B-Don's tombstone in Lake View Cemetery with a bottle of Jameson stout and two shot glasses. The inscription read, "Beloved friend, brother, and bartender. Brendon B-Don Wheeler 1972–2023." Someone had put a tip jar on top of the grave. This made me laugh in the quiet and somber atmosphere of the cemetery. I reflected for a moment on all that had happened. I couldn't quite decide if I was happy or if I was numb.

I put the shot glasses on top of the tombstone and uncorked the bottle. I poured a small amount out on the grave. B-Don wouldn't want me wasting too much good whiskey. I poured two shots.

"Cheers, brother. You know the guy that ruined our concert? Well, he is sleeping with the fishes. I set him on fire in a parking garage in Paris a few days ago. I know that doesn't sound like me, but I have changed over the last little bit. I met this girl. You know, the one with the green eyes from the bar. She wrecked my world, man."

I smiled and picked up the shot glass. I clinked it against his.

"Cheers, you know all the corny toasts that I do, so this is less fun, but here's to seeing you soon."

"Not too soon. Or I myself will forever sleep and come clap your cheeks for eternity," a voice said from behind me.

A hand slipped into my grasp as I turned.

"This is her." I motioned her forward. "She is the cause of and solution to all of life's problems."

I got a small punch in the arm, but I swear I could hear B-Don laughing from the beyond. I reached into my pocket and removed two .45 ACP spent shell casings. The first one I put on B-Don's tombstone. I began to cry quietly. After a few moments, I realized that I was not crying for my friend anymore. I was mourning the kind, merciful, and thoughtful person he inspired me to be. The second casing I handed to Ariel. Her face had been scarred and changed by the sniper's bullet, but she still looked perfect to me. I traced a finger along the massive pink-and-white scar.

"Does it hurt?" I asked.

She shook her head. "No, not as much as it did after my...I don't know, sixth surgery."

Ariel moved her long black hair over her right eye. I could tell it made her self-conscious.

I swept the hair out of the way and pulled her close to me.

"You know I love it, right? Your scar, I mean. It's sexy."

I gave her a little kiss on her right cheek right in the middle of the scar.

She shook her head. "I'm deformed now. I am still coming to terms with that."

"Well, you always did look a little lopsided before. I think that round evened you out."

For this comment, I received a not-so-loving punch in the arm.

"Ow, woman, what do you want from me?"

She smiled. I could tell this action hurt her. "Not much. To quote a great philosopher, watch my back when it's dark. Call me on my bullshit when it's needed. Feed me awesome food. Love me till the end of time? Or we can just go home either way."

I smiled. "Which great philosopher said that?"

Ariel shook her head and said, "Come on, Mr. Senior Florist."

Smiling at the first official use of my new title, we moved back toward KITT, who was parked at the bottom of the hill.

"How is Doc doing by the way?"

Ariel smiled. "You know Doc, always having a good time. Arrangements by Boris is up and running, causing no end of pain for our enemies on the other side of the world. Being in charge suits him."

"Well, Vidar, what is next for us?"

"After we find and kill Alecto, I think everything goes back to normal. The world's geopolitical situation notwithstanding, I think our lives are going to get very simple. Evil man, dead man."

I nodded and hoped that maybe one day, after a river of blood and a pile of bodies had been made, with hopefully a mountain and ocean saved, maybe then Ariel and I could retire together and live a quiet life. That was for later. My fear is that it would never be later. I kissed Ariel's forehead as we three watched the sun sink into the Seattle skyline.

— *Epilogue* —

OTHAN SAT IN THE lobby of Valhol coffee and imports, stirring a mixture of coffee, cream, and sugar on the table. He was reading an intelligence report from the Azrael. Ariel had it sent to him earlier that morning. It was a briefing on the actions of Dmitri Mendeleyev, his former friend and confidant. The fact that Dmitri betrayed them was not in question. The question Azrael had was how. It looked like the former KGB spook had figured out how to remove his chip.

Othan smiled and thought, *Well, he wasn't the first, and he won't be the last.*

Othan thought quietly about the whole situation. There were some things that just weren't adding up.

Why would you betray us for three million, Dmitri. You didn't need the money...unless you did.

Othan had a thought and typed an e-mail to a friend who was a forensics accountant: *Need information on the attached file. Get me what you can send me an invoice.*

A thumbs-up emoji returned to Othan's phone seconds later.

"Freyr, bring me another coffee when you have a moment, please."

The man behind the counter with the red beard nodded and said, "At once, Vidar."

The front door to the coffee shop opened, and an older man in a tailored suit that had a Christian cross as a tie tack walked to the front register.

"A flat white please, with cane sugar."

The man's accent was slight, but Othan recognized it as Easter European.

Freyr nodded and began working on the concoction. The man threw a hundred-dollar bill on the counter and walked toward Othan's table. Steel slid against Kydex as Freyr's pistol leveled at the back of the old man's head. He was still steaming the milk with his left hand.

Othan smiled and motioned for Freyr to put his pistol away.

"It's okay, Freyr, I have been expecting Mr. Alecto for some time now."

Freyr looked angry and ready to squeeze the trigger. "Yes, sir." He put his pistol away and continued making his coffee.

"I have waited some time to meet you, Othan."

Othan motioned to the seat across from him. "Have you now? And why is that? Everyone knows where to find me."

Aldrich Alecto sat down across from the old spymaster and spoke.

"Well, not everyone. The only reason I am here is to make a truce with your daughter's company."

Othan held his hands wide. "I'm retired. How could I be of help?"

The older man said, "Don't fuck with me, Vidar. I have done a little research since this little dance began. Tell your daughter that I want a sit-down at a place of her choosing, just us, in public."

Freyr mean mugged the old man as he sat the man's flat white and Othan's coffee down on the table.

Othan smiled sadly. "I will tell her. A small piece of advice if you'll have it. You are already dead, Mr. Alecto. There is a bullet or a pill or some other calamity with your name on it. You can run, hide, fight, or bargain. It won't matter. The bell tolls, and it tolls for thee."

Aldrich threw his flat white across the room, where it shattered against the wall.

"God help me, what is better, Othan, to have a dead enemy or a live ally that is highly placed, one that could help solve certain problems? Also, I don't think I am as easy to kill as you say, or your barista over there would have pulled the trigger."

Othan smiled at the man's outburst. "Bargaining is the third stage of grief. It sounds like you only have two more to go. It would be interesting to know whether you complete all five stages before or after my daughter puts an ice pick through your skull."

Aldrich folded his hands. "Well, in that case. I suppose I must take my leave. What would you do if you were me?"

Othan picked up his coffee and gave it a small sip. "Oh, if it were me? I would kick and scream as I was dragged into my grave."

Aldrich smiled at this he stood and started toward the back door. "I appreciate the advice."

Othan smiled. "Well, that's all I am good for these days."

Aldrich moved toward the backdoor seemingly in a hurry. "Goodbye, Othan."

Othan smiled, knowing that the man would get his sit-down. But only one of them would leave that sit-down alive.

"Goodbye, Mr. Alecto."

The old man left without another word. The way he said goodbye bothered Othan for some reason. Othan thought about where the old man had walked while he was in the small coffee shop. Othan felt under the table, and a large brick of something was under the side Aldrich has been sitting. Othan popped the object off and saw that it was a large block of plastic explosive, probably CEMTEX. With a cell phone attached to it, the screen showed a countdown. Four seconds.

Othan screamed, "Freyr, run!" The man behind the counter complied. Othan threw the C4 toward the front door, but he knew it wouldn't matter.

A few moments later, an electronic laugh started warbling from the cell phone attached to the block of explosives. Othan walked over to the device and saw a message on the phone. It read: *She can call me from this phone. Number is programmed in. Don't take too long.*

Othan relaxed, but felt silly that he had let the man come and go freely. Othan picked up his cell phone and dialed the number for Arrangements by Ariel.

www.ingramcontent.com/pod-product-compliance
Lightning Source LLC
Chambersburg PA
CBHW021958271224
19559CB00028B/439